COMMANDER GALLANT

H. Peter Alesso

THE HENRY GALLANT SAGA

Midshipman Henry Gallant in Space © 2013
Lieutenant Henry Gallant © 2014
Henry Gallant and the *Warrior* © 2015
Commander Gallant © 2020
Captain Henry Gallant © 2019
Commodore Henry Gallant © 2020
Henry Gallant and the Great Ship © 2020

Other Novels by H. Peter Alesso

Captain Hawkins © 2016
Dark Genius © 2017
Youngblood © 2018

COMMANDER GALLANT

This is a work of fiction. All characters and events portrayed in this book are fictional, and any resemblance to real people or incidents is purely coincidental.

VSL Publications
Pleasanton, CA 94566
www.videosoftwarelab.com

Edition 1.00

ISBN-13: 9798560297039

A warrior must know himself

before he can understand his enemy.

GLIESE STAR SYSTEM

Gleise-581 is a M-class red dwarf—smaller, cooler, and less massive than Sol at about 20 light-years distance.

Five planets:

Planet Alpha is at 1.7 AU (astronomical units). It takes 3.15 days to complete an orbit. It's a composite of a carbonaceous, silicate, and metal-rich rock covering a barren volcanic mantle.

Planet Beta is within the habitable liquid methane zone. Capable of supporting the methane lifeform. It is the aliens' home world. It is a ringed planet wrapped in a cloak of hydrocarbon smog suspended in its nitrogen-rich atmosphere.

Planet Gamma is similar to Beta.

Planet Delta is a gas giant composed of hydrogen and helium with numerous volcanic methane moons, much like our Neptune.

Planet Epsilon, at 5.5 AU, is a low-mass planet with a climate model like Venus.

The asteroid disk is at 15.8 AU

Titan—Home Fleet

36 Battlecruisers
196 Cruisers
688 Destroyers
1688 Auxiliary Support Ships

Titan Planetary Defenses

124 Orbiting Battle Stations
220 Ground Missile Bases
100,000 Commercial ships

CONTENTS

CHAPTER 1

Methane Planet

As the warp bubble collapsed, the *Warrior* popped out on the edge of the Gliese-581star system. The *Warrior* was Captain Henry Gallant's first command, the culmination of everything he'd worked for since entering the academy. With a rocket-shaped hull over one hundred meters long, she boasted stealth technology, a sub-light antimatter engine, and an FTL dark-matter drive.

Gallant gawked. "What an awesome sight."

The busy bridge crew stole their eyes away from their instrument panels long enough to gaze in amazement at the Titan civilization. The many ships traveling between planets were remarkable, but the energy readings of the densely populated planets were off the charts.

From his command chair, Gallant focused on the home of his alien enemy. The star was an M-class red dwarf—smaller, cooler, and less massive than Sol, at about twenty light-years from Earth.

"Sir," said the astrogator, "we're three light-days from the sun. Five planets are visible."

"It's like the solar system," marveled Midshipman Stedman, an eager but green officer. His slight build and round, boyish face often seemed to get lost amid the bustle of the more experienced crew.

"If you don't notice that the sun is ruby instead of amber and that there are only five planets," chided Chief Howard. The oldest member of the crew, he was a seasoned veteran with a slight potbelly. He wore his immaculate uniform with pride. Every ribbon, insignia, and star on his left breast had a long and glorious story. He was only too glad to retell the stories—with appropriate embellishments—over a whiskey, preferably Jack Daniels.

The astrogator said, "Only two planets are within the liquid methane zone. But some of the asteroids and moons may have been methane-formed."

"Wow, the system is full of mining colonies, military bases, and communications satellites. The spaceship traffic is amazing. There must be many thousands of ships," said Stedman.

The astrogator reported, "Scans on the second and third planets show billions of beings. The second planet has the greatest energy density. I'll bet that's their planet of origin."

"Quite likely," acknowledged Gallant, his curiosity aroused.

"An imposing presence, Skipper," said Roberts. Young and garrulous, Roberts had steady nerves and sound professional judgment. He was of average height with brown hair, a lean, smooth face, and a sturdy body. Gallant had come to trust him as a stalwart friend—something one only discovers during a crisis. That moment had come several months earlier when Roberts put his career and his life on the line for Gallant.

"It has one large moon," added Chief Howard.

Gliese-Beta was a majestic ringed planet wrapped in a dense hydrocarbon nitrogen-rich atmosphere. It was opaque to blue light but transparent to red and infrared. The red dwarf's infrared warmed the planet and made it habitable for methane lifeforms. Gliese-Gamma was similar.

The astrogator continued, "The next two planets are gas giants with several moons. Gliese-Delta is composed of hydrogen and helium with volcanic methane moons, much like our Neptune. Gliese-Epsilon is a low-mass planet with a climate model like a runaway greenhouse effect—analogous to our Venus."

"That's interesting," said Roberts.

Encouraged, the astrogator concluded his report, "The system includes a disk-shaped asteroid field."

The *Warrior* used its radars and telescopes to plot the planets' orbits. The CIC team computed the course of nearby contacts. The *Warrior's* emission spectrum was controlled in stealth mode.

"What's your assessment of their military strength?" asked Gallant.

The CIC team listed the large and small warships, followed by planetary defenses. They added an estimate of the traffic flow. It was a long list.

OOD said, "Here is the compiled reported, sir."

"Very well," acknowledged Gallant as he scanned the tablet.

The sub-light engines drove the ship onward into the heart of the system.

Calculating their flight path, the astrogator reported, "We'll reach the asteroids in about forty-eight hours, sir."

Gallant tapped the screen to call up the AI settings for plot control and touched the destination. He ordered a deep-space probe sent toward the largest asteroids.

"It'll take several hours to start transmitting, sir."

Gallant said, "Once we get a base established, we can go deeper into their system. I'm interested in seeing how their home planet differs from our solar system. We need to learn about their society and leadership structure."

Roberts asked, "Skipper, we've always called them Titans, but what do they call themselves?"

Gallant said, "I can't replicate their name in our language. As autistic savants, their communication is different from our speech. We'll continue to call them Titans."

The CIC team reported, "Our initial assessment shows that Gliese-Beta has a diverse topology and climate. It's ecologically rich with many species. Extensive methane oceans and landmasses have abundant soil and temperature conditions. It can support a wide variety of methane-breathing lifeforms."

Roberts said, "It's so different from our water-rich Earth."

"Earth is mostly water," said Gallant. "The oceans provide us with fish to eat, water vapor to fill our skies with clouds, rain to nurture our crops, and water for us to drink. Our metabolism and food cycle are water-based, and we ourselves are 97 percent water. For us, water is life."

"How does this methane world sustain the Titans?" asked Roberts

Gallant said, "The temperature variations provide methane in all three phases: gas, liquid, and solid. Methane rivers freeze at high latitudes to form polar sheets. The methane cycle is a complex molecular soup. It is formed from reactions when the ultraviolet radiation from the sun strikes the methane. Their methane life forms are comparable to our oxygen-based life cycle. And just as methane is a poison to us, oxygen is toxic to them."

Roberts asked, "Are they autistic savants because of the methane-based chemistry?"

"That's one of the things we're here to learn. Our first task is to establish a base," said Gallant. "From that hideout, the *Warrior* can recharge her stealth battery and remain safe between operations."

Maintaining stealth mode, the *Warrior* approached the outer edge of the asteroid belt. She conducted a spiral search to map the interrelated defenses. The crew looked for an asteroid large enough to hide the ship.

Gallant and the XO combed through the CIC data to check for potential locations.

"How about here, sir?" asked one of the analysts, pointing to a cluster near the outer perimeter of the field. The asteroid belt included many asymmetrical rocky bodies. Three smaller clusters skirted the outer edge. Some asteroids were more than one kilometer wide.

"Yes, that might do," said Gallant. "It's large enough to block radar detection and shield us from view while we're recharging. We'll call this base Alamo."

Gallant ordered a two-man team to construct a relay station on the asteroid. He left one of the *Warrior's* remote-controlled drones on the surface along with a supply depot.

Once Alamo was established, he settled the *Warrior* into orbit behind the rocks to recharge her stealth batteries.

The next day, they reconnoitered the fifth planet and discovered a communication junction box. Moving deeper into Titan territory, they caught a bird's-eye view of the alien's home planet. They saw several orbiting shipyards and space stations.

The *Warrior* collected information about the Titan fleet and civilization. The bridge crew was surprised at the incredible infrastructure the aliens had developed. Operating in such a populated environment was a challenge, but the cloaking technology allowed the *Warrior* to remain undetected.

What followed were busy days as the *Warrior* peered into the inner workings of the Titan system. The crew compiled detailed lists of warships and their deposition, as well as their refueling and patrolling pattern. They learned shipping traffic patterns, monitored the industrial capacity, and accumulated population statistics. There were over twenty billion inhabitants. The Titans had built their main military headquarters on the third planet. It had a layered defense with satellites, minefields, and overlapping fortresses. A display showed fluctuating energy emissions for their industry.

After two weeks of collecting information, Roberts approached Gallant's command chair. He asked, "Captain, can you give us your game plan going forward?"

Gallant recalled Admiral Collingsworth's orders detailing their hazardous mission. All of which required his stealth ship and crew to be at peak operational and battle readiness.

He said, "Yes. It's time to fill you in. We've collected a lot of info, but scouting isn't our sole mission. I intend to do more. Much more."

The bridge crew leaned closer, eager to drink in every tidbit of juicy news.

He said, "We are finally ready to engage in asymmetric warfare. We will penetrate the Titan communication network to learn about their military deployment."

He paused for dramatic effect as everyone drew

in a deep breath. "And we will raid commercial shipping to throw their civilian population into turmoil."

A buzz of excitement filled the bridge.

"That's a tall order, Skipper," said Roberts.

"Yes, it is." Gallant asked, "Are you up for it?"

"Can do, sir!" said Roberts.

"Can do, sir!" roared the bridge crew.

Commander Julie Ann McCall stepped out of CIC and onto the bridge. She walked straight to Gallant and grabbed his arm.

She said, "I must speak to you immediately."

McCall was not a line officer. She was a product of genetic engineering who had inherited tendencies of the most diabolical kind, which made her a talented Solar Intelligence Agency (SIA) operative. Her considerable skills in manipulation and deception had fostered her brilliant career. What she lacked in kindness and empathy, she more than made up for in intellect, guile, and allure. She was astonishingly efficient at analyzing an opponent's flaws. Some who had felt her cold-blooded sting labeled her a sociopath who would do anything to achieve her goals.

Gallant's long and checkered relationship with her remained a riddle to him.

Now he gazed into her blazing eyes, and then he looked down at her hand on his arm.

She pulled her hand away but repeated, "I need to speak with you privately."

The commotion on the bridge died down and the two senior officers became the focus of attention.

Gallant rose from his command chair, and said,

"Commander, please come with me."

All eyes on the bridge followed the pair as they left.

CHAPTER 2

It's on Your Head

Gallant's tiny cabin was the perfect pressure cooker for the anger boiling within him. But before he could vent his temper, McCall said, "Please accept my apology."

He stood in the recess of the confined space and glared at her.

"I should never have put my hand on you, especially not on the bridge. It was a flagrant breach of protocol. I am sorry for that. Please accept my apology."

He let his emotions dissipate.

"Apology accepted."

He decided to hear her complaint. He said, "Are you taking issue with this ship's mission, Commander?"

She tilted her head to one side. "Captain Gallant, I have a copy of your orders. Your statement on the bridge does not conform to them."

Gallant sat down on the only chair in the room. He leaned against his desk.

McCall visibly relaxed. She pulled down a flap of flat metal from the bulkhead. She wiggled onto the uncomfortable makeshift chair.

He touched the safe, which held his orders but made no effort to open it.

"I disagree," he said.

She said, "Your orders state that the *Warrior* is to perform a reconnaissance of the Gliese star system. It's to collect as much military intelligence as possible."

"Yes."

"Those orders do not authorize commerce raiding."

"They permit asymmetric warfare operation in the furtherance of intelligence collection."

"That's true. But that means operations that benefit data collection—not destroying ships."

"By conducting limited commercial raiding attacks, we will test the enemy's response and ability to adapt. We will force them to move military units and expose more of their tactical operations. We will gain far more intelligence by rattling their cage a little than if we passively travel around the star system and leave."

"What do you intend?"

He said, "Over many centuries, the tale of a raider is the story of how weaker navies fight back. The raider offers not only real military value but great psychological effect. A raider confronts an

enemy of greater strength, so it must adopt unortho-
dox tactics. Its threat to destroy commercial traffic
required hunters to search endlessly for them. A commercial raider lets the enemy know she's out there.
So, they must send out hunter-killer groups. Our
scoreboard of ships destroyed or captured may be
great or small but is nonetheless dangerous. Raiders
disrupt normal commercial operations and disturb
civilian tranquility."

"That is not in your primary mission description," she countered.

"The location of the raider cannot be taken for
granted. They must provide wide protection and remain ever alert. The actual explosion of weapons is
less effective than the uncertainty the raider gener-
ates. Ultimately, raiders can produce orders of magnitude of trouble."

"I still don't see how . . ."

He cut in, "Once we've stirred things up, we
will penetrate their communication networks. There
we can gather military intelligence on how they are
reacting and what measures they are taking. It will be
a gold mine of intelligence on their deployment and
reactions. As an SIA operative, you should be especially pleased."

"What if you're rattling-the-cage gets the *Warrior* destroyed? Then the United Planets will never
get all the data we've already collected."

"The static intel we've acquired so far is mere
statistics—numbers of ships, energy output, popula-
tions, and traffic routes. Those numbers don't win

wars. Any other recon ship can gather that. We can use drones to collect it and transmit later."

He stood and leaned against the bulkhead. "By perturbing the military leadership, we gain the opportunity to obtain actionable intelligence on their performance and strategic thinking. Everything we accumulate after that will be much more valuable."

McCall looked troubled. She spent a moment lost in thought.

She said, "You make a cogent point, but there is a great risk."

"Ours is a risky business. I must balance the risk against reward. I promise you I will make every effort to conduct raids with minimum peril and maximum payoff."

McCall remained quiet for a moment.

He continued, "I understand my responsibility to this ship and its crew, and I will not put them in harm's way unnecessarily, but we will complete this mission."

"I've made my concerns known," said McCall. "Now, it's on your head."

CHAPTER 3

A Promising Beginning

T here was something hypnotic about the eerie midwatch aboard the *Warrior*. Even the AI computer seemed trapped in a recursive loop.

For a long unremarkable moment, Gallant gazed around the bridge.

The viewscreen showed the alien planets lost inside the vast star system. The alien worlds were unknown and unexplored, but Gallant wanted to change that. The light of distant stars twinkled in contrast to the dots on the viewscreen. It might seem like a lot of empty space, but it was teeming with activity. Ships slithered through the cold dark space toward locations near and far. But, despite the great diversity of destinations, there were distinct traffic patterns.

Gallant glanced around him at the subdued midwatch activities within the *Warrior*. There was little maintenance or repair work, but everyone was eager to get on with their job.

Tall and gangly, Lieutenant Clay was reviewing the contacts. His solemn eyes ran through targets that might prove to be a problem.

Chief Howard was tapping his fingers absentmindedly on a row of steel levers next to his watch station.

The helmsman was exerting minimal pressure against the helm to keep it perfectly aligned.

The sensor operator was listening and watching, scanning the data scrolling across his screen.

Other watch standers were exhibiting a daydream-like state of casual awareness.

Yet, Gallant had no doubt they would all spring into a professional tempo the moment a threat was detected.

Gallant ordered, "Officer of the Deck, keep us clear of the high traffic areas."

"Aye aye, sir," said Clay. He stepped close to the astrogator and gazed at the navigation plot. It showed the *Warrior* a mere eight light-hours from Gliese-Beta in the heart of the star system. It was no surprise that the Titans had a thriving commerce business between planets. The first area of operation was a step into a larger plan of movements choreographed to optimize the threat of the *Warrior*.

"Chief Howard, how is our stealth charge doing?" asked Gallant.

Howard's roly-poly cheeks broke into a wide grin. "Just fine, sir. We're at 88.7 percent. I reckon we have five days operating at this rate before we need to return to Alamo."

"Very well," said Gallant.

He tracked and plotted shipping lanes and traffic he wanted a light traffic area for his first encounter. He tracked a good target. He identified it as a large freighter. He set an intercept course.

"We have a close contact," said the sensor operator. "They're following the traffic route, sir."

Gallant asked, "Which contact?"

"Tango 142 is bearing 156 mark 2, range five light-minutes," reported the sensor operator.

"Very well," said Clay. He glanced at Gallant awaiting new instruction. "Sir, Tango 142 is the target you selected. Do you want to set an intercept course?"

Gallant nodded, "Officer of the Deck, change course to intercept Tango 142."

Tango 142 was a small cargo craft. One of the thousands that the *Warrior* was tracking. It was bad luck that it was the farthest from the main traffic lane to Gliese-Beta.

"Change course to intercept Tango 142, aye aye, sir" replied Clay. "Helm, come to course 166 mark 2."

"Come to course 166 mark 2, aye aye, sir," responded the helmsman.

A moment later, the helmsman reported, "On course 166 mark 2, sir."

"Very well," said Clay. "Captain, we will intercept Tango 142 in seventeen minutes."

"Very well," said Gallant as the *Warrior* approached its first victim. He asked, "Officer of the

Deck, how many contacts will be within one light-hour when we intercept?"

"Twenty-seven, sir. But none will be within thirty light-minutes."

"Thank you. That will be acceptable. Sound general quarters."

CLANG! CLANG! CLANG!

The crew of the *Warrior* hurried to their stations.

In record time, Chief Howard reported, "All stations manned and ready, sir."

Clay responded, "Very well."

When the *Warrior* was within thirty light-seconds of the commercial ship, Gallant said, "Drop cloak. Target a warning shot at Tango 142 with railgun-1."

The weapons officer reported, "Railgun-1 has a weapon's lock on Tango 142 plus one light-second, sir."

"Fire."

The Titan cargo ship began transmitting a distress signal. Escape pods ejected from the ship.

"Do you want to send a boarding party, sir?" asked the OOD.

"Yes. I don't believe that civilian ships will self-destruct like the Titan military ships. There may be some communication devices onboard we can use. Send a team."

"Aye aye, sir."

After firing at the ship and signaling it to surrender, the civilian crew ejected in escape pods and let him board their ship without destruction. This was not what they had encountered with a military ship, which self-destructed. They boarded the ship twelve hours later for safety. They search for documents and communication equipment.

The sensor operator provided updates on all ships in the area. They were all scattered away from the victim. None were approaching.

The team made the round trip in under thirty minutes and found a few interesting items.

The sensor operator reported, "One ship is on an intercept course. Fifteen light-minutes away."

"Very well," said Gallant. "Officer of the Deck raise stealth. Ahead flank. Get us out of the area."

The *Warrior* captured two more small cargo ships the next day. The commercial ships had no defense, and the *Warrior* scooped up supplies and information. The Titan crews used escape pods.

The *Warrior* remained nearby for several hours while they collected their booty, then she accelerated away. The Titans had sent a distress call, but Gallant was quick to move away to other areas before the enemy could react.

The *Warrior*'s crew was justifiably proud of its first steps as a raider. Gallant considered it a significant triumph, modest though it was. His strategy was governed by the ship's capabilities. Stealth was its foremost advantage, along with its ability to secretly recharge. Its armament was slight compared to the enemy but not insignificant thanks to the FASER. As a raider, they enjoyed the initiative. The *Warrior* could choose its area of operations and shift it constantly to keep the enemy off balance.

Gallant sat in his command chair, lost in thought while the bridge crew chatted quietly about the situation.

"What else can we do?" asked Clay.

Roberts said, "The skipper will come up with something novel; you can bet on that."

"We're close to Beta-Gliese," commented Clay.

The viewscreen showed the nearby ships included cargo, transport, ore, and supply ships. Near the planet were shuttles interplanetary tugs. CIC detected starfighter bases, sensor arrays, and space stations; all were duly noted.

"The best place to start operations. Once we raise hell here, we and move on to less dangerous locations, but the Titans won't know where we are," said Howard.

Roberts said, "I'll bet they move everything they got here. We won't get this close again."

"That's perfectly true," said Howard, "but we wouldn't have to. We'll be on to an easier target."

"What would that be?" asked the helmsman. "We're already doing more than I thought was possible."

"Don't use your limited measuring rod when talking about the captain. He has a unique ability to torment the Titans," chuckled Roberts.

"Well, what do *you* think he'll do?"

Roberts wasn't sure enough to offer an opinion. The difficulty was no one had Gallant's imagination and drive.

"I think we'll be as surprised as the Titans," said Howard.

The chuckles and whispers finally wrestled Gallant from his preoccupation.

He asked, "Mr. Roberts, how are your proficiency boards progressing?"

John Roberts said, "I'm not as far along as I'd like, sir. You know, with one thing and another demanding my time aboard the ship, it's hard to find time for personal items."

"Your professional development is as much a ship requirement as the antimatter engines. You must make time to keep up with your proficiency. You'll need to qualify for command before long."

On the one hand, every lieutenant dreamed of promotion and command. It was in their blood. Otherwise, they wouldn't be valuable officers. The metamorphosis from junior officer to command does not happen overnight. The transformation takes planning, effort and training. Promotion to command was as rare as the ships they sought. Besides sweat and talent, promotion needed good fortune and, sometimes, a nudge from a benefactor.

On the other hand, heroic action and brilliant tactics might do just as well. Every officer yearned for command, but the chances often went through seniority in the chain of command. Roberts was always an active subordinate. Worthy of command.

Roberts said, "I'll keep that in mind, sir. Next time I'll inspecting a ruptured compartment tank or reviewing a disassembled oxygen generator." He stood stiffly, trying to avoid Gallant's eyes. A bit of prickling perspiration slid down his collar.

"Mister Roberts, do I detect a twinge of sarcasm in your tone?" Gallant flickered one eyebrow at him for dramatic effect. There was something in his stare that drew attention. It was impossible to read Gallant's internal struggle to control his laughter, but his broad smile allowed the bridge crew to chuckle. It was rare when they saw their captain expressed open humor.

With that, Roberts grinned and returned to his duties. He was eager to get his daily responsibilities finished so he could work late into the night on his proficiency exams. He displayed a renewed sense of effort. There were a few minutes of grace left to him to get things done.

After a week of raiding, Gallant asked McCall to the wardroom to discuss operations. She was on top of her game and detailed that the Titans were now aware they had a dangerous adversary in their mist. The *Warrior* had spent days collecting transmissions to decode and translate. McCall and her spooks examined the information. She evaluated the military resources.

She said, "Your single ship has startled the Titans and caused anxiety. The *Warrior* has enjoyed a period of success, but soon countermeasures will start to take effect."

"What do you expect the Titans to do?"

She said, "The Titan command will probably initiate plans to track events. They don't know yet how many raiders there are. They could start convoys, sent out reconnaissance scouts, and deploy additional sensors arrays."

"I'm not worried. Our stealth is capable."

She said, "They will also send hunter-killer teams."

Gallant nodded.

She offered a handcrafted plan for further intelligence collection, including ideas of locations to exploit and others to avoid.

"That sounds sensible," he said. He marshaled his thoughts for a minute and reordered his thinking based upon her suggestions. He had his ideas in order now and rattled them off in quick succession. The words sprang from his mouth, almost without consent. He was eager to reach an agreement.

He said, "We can improve our game by sending out drones, laying mines, and constructing relay stations. I have plans to attack a small outpost and let them broadcast distress signals."

"All of that will increase the pressure on the Titans," said McCall.

She moved closer and spoke softly, "But it will also increase the risk."

CHAPTER 4

A Deadly Turn

For three weeks, the *Warrior* rampaged through the star system, capturing, or destroying, two or three commercial ships a day. It darted around from one planet to the next, leaving behind a confusing pattern that Gallant was certain would bewilder the Titans.

So far, the *Warrior* had destroyed forty-nine ships, damaged twelve, and scattered numerous convoys. She eluded the hunters. There were many conflicting reports about her location, so the *Warrior* remained a mystery.

Gallant kept his crew busy disguising the ship's emissions to give the impression that there was more than one raider. He hoped the enemy would underestimate the problems of shadowing his ship. He sent out drones that emitted signals to station buoys. The buoy signals would then mislead the Titan trackers.

The Titan civilian news broadcasts indicated

that the war had arrived at their doorstep. They reported that there were scores of raiders. Fleet ships were dispatched to protect the commercial lifeblood of the civilization. Civilian protection was ramped up across trillions of cubic kilometers of space. It was a vast drain of resources.

As the *Warrior* moved, its presence was like waving a red flag at the bull. As soon as she captured a ship, the Titan patrols would swarm to attack, only to find that the *Warrior* had slipped past their net. Gallant often left some captured cargo ships behind, broadcasting a distress signal.

The *Warrior* trekked through the system and waited for new prospects, but the Titans were getting smart. Gallant need to get more information about the enemy's deployment, but he was pleased with hoodwinking the Titans.

The *Warrior* returned to the charging station and recharged and upgraded some equipment several times.

Gallant said, "Mister Roberts go on recounting your story about the attack on the outpost."

"My team landed," said Roberts. "I sent two scouts ahead. The rest followed."

Gallant leaned closer over the wardroom table. The officers around the room listened intently. Everyone was excited about the expedition.

"There was no serious opposition."

"Then what?"

"I deployed the team around the main structure. After a moment, I sent them in. There was no resistance. We secured two civilian prisoners who surrendered without a fuss. We recovered some communication equipment and a library of data," concluded Roberts.

"Roberts' success in gathering information on ship movements is a good advantage," said McCall. Then she furrowed her brow and said, "This is the sixth year of the war, and prospects for resolution remain unsettled. No one can predict when, if ever, the suffering will end, but this a mission is a step in that direction. I applaud Roberts' success."

Gallant looked at her, trying to gauge her musings and wondering whether her doubts were sincere or intended to provoke a response. He said, "Our job is to stay hidden and gather information to improve our chances of waging war. The *Warrior* is perfectly designed for this. Its stealth and high performance will let us go everywhere they don't want us to be. When we're done, we shall know the enemy."

"We all volunteered for this," said McCall. "As spies and raiders, we are the lonely sentries on the frontline against the Titan. Nevertheless, I continue to advise caution. One wrong move now could prove fatal."

Gallant worked with CIC to break codes and

plot the traffic. Pulling all this information together, he was able to gain insight into opportunities for raiding. It allowed him to avoid sensor arrays and detection.

The commercial ships varied in size and speed, but none carried armament or shielding. The crews varied from a dozen to several scores. It was a raider's paradise. The information about the hunter-killer groups allowed Gallant to plot a safe passage to and from targets.

Ultimately, he hoped for a breakdown of the Titan leadership.

The newscasters' sanguine voices over the communication channels spoke of normal traffic news and demands for products. That changed when the frequent updates about the raiders increased.

Gallant was pleased with his dissembling. He even tried to emulate a Titan destroyers' signals at one point to sneak up on a convoy. He simulated an attack on another outpost.

After several weeks, the *Warrior* returned to Alamo to recharged. But they never stayed long. They were anxious to resume their hunt for targets of opportunity.

There were many ships plying between planets. One of Gallants favorite tricks was for the *Warrior* to capture a ship and copied its emergency transponder to call for help. He sent drones to call for help at different spots and times. He broadcast warnings throughout the system.

The *Warrior's* tactics of scouting, identifying a

suitable target, and executing an attack, had become routine. So, when the sensor operator reported a fresh target, Tango 923, the bridge crew responded casually.

The ship changed course as the *Warrior* dropped cloak and approached. The Titan began zigzagging.

Gallant changed course to intercept. He maneuvered the *Warrior* closer and decelerated to match the vessel's velocity.

There was something troubling about this ship. Gallant began to wonder if this target was different. He wasn't given to flights of imagination, but he conjured a concern.

Tango 923 isn't working hard enough to escape.

Tango 923 wasn't panicking or fleeing as was normally the case.

Something was very wrong.

Gallant wondered, *Is this a trap?*

Tango 923 changed course, again. It turned directly at the *Warrior* with its rail guns and lasers blasting.

Belatedly, Gallant said, "Sound general quarters."

CLANG! CLANG! CLANG!

Tango 923 was one of the more imaginative Titan responses to its raider problem. It was a Q-ship. It appeared as a vulnerable merchantman but carried hidden armaments, making it as powerful as a destroyer.

Gallant ordered, "Weapons; target Tango 923."

The weapons officer trained his targeting scope on the Q-ship. The enemy's elevation and bearing were transmitted into the AI analyzer to train the rail gun on the target. This aiming process and feedback produced excellent hits.

Stedman commanded the rail gun station. He ordered the gunners for batteries A and B, "Prepare to fire in unison."

Both turrets A and B revolved to the set bearing and fired. Each breach was loaded in the tube. The projectiles were a mix of solid metal and explosive core. The layer pressed the trigger, and the electric current moved the turret. He saw the ready light turn green.

"Rail guns ready, sir," reported Stedman.

"Open fire."

Stedman glanced at the gunner and said, "Shoot!"

A deadly stream of metal projectile shells was sent at the target with a mix of 'hot' shells that radioed back the trajectory info. The feedback shells updated the targeting analysis.

The projectiles were mostly solid heavy metals. Every third one was packed with explosives. This was the most effective weapon against a ship without shields.

The rail gun barrels were heating up as the firing continued. Each projectile was loaded from a hoist pulling the shells from the armory. Each broadside took several seconds to reload and direct the barrel.

Stedman adjusted the bearing repeatedly based upon the hot shell updates. He focused his aim on the midship.

He repeated, "Shoot!

The Q-ship was also firing lasers and projectiles at the *Warrior*, but its salvo was deflected by the *Warrior's* shield. Several shells did manage to penetrate but they bounced off the titanium hull. Damage control teams quickly took care of any problems. The Q-ship hoped to delay the *Warrior* long enough for help to arrive.

A minute later, *Warrior* scored serious damage to the Q-ship.

Gallant turned the *Warrior* and sped away under cloak.

The Q-ship's attempt to follow were futile.

"That was too close," said McCall.

"We need better intelligence about the Titan's deployment," said Gallant. "And I know how to get it."

CHAPTER 5

Wasp

Gallant sat patiently as Stedman maneuvered the two-man Wasp into a low orbit around the small moon near Gliese-Epsilon. They settled near the communication satellite hub. Protected by its stealth technology, the ship flew over the complex. Stedman identified a good landing site and set the ship down. He looked pleased with his effort despite a last-minute bump.

"That was acceptable," said Gallant. "With practice, you'll do better."

He unstrapped from his seat and said, "At the data transmitter, I'll install a bug to tap the data feed. As soon as you receive a steady data flow, retransmit it to the *Warrior*. Once they confirm we have a good lock, I'll set the monitoring device to automatic and return. Do you understand?"

"Yes, sir."

Gallant strapped on his jetpack and stepped

out. The starlight offered faint illumination, but as the moon rotated, light from the sun crept over the area.

He bounced over the jagged surface for about twenty minutes, keeping a lookout for sentries. The rocky surface slowed his progress but luckily wasn't a serious impediment. The larger boulders offered cover. At one point, he saw a Titan patrol. He dropped into a shallow gully.

At the junction box, it took several times before he got a reliable data feed.

The pair repeated the process at several other junction boxes. They gained confidence as they progressed to other satellites.

Gallant observed Stedman knowing he had placed a great burden on the midshipman. Stedman was well-balanced and quick to adapt. His skill level soon advanced beyond novice. Gallant found himself relying on the eager young man.

On the moon of the fourth planet, Gliese-Delta, Gallant said, "I'll be attempting something different here. Instead of stealing data, I'm going to set up a mental link into the communication network and listen to the Titan communication. Hopefully, I too will learn more with practice."

Gallant set up the neural link and connected to the alien network interface. After a few minutes, the monitoring AI system challenged him.

The AI access controller asked him, "Who are you?"

Gallant had prepared a ruse he hoped would trick the computer.

He said, "I am a citizen pretending to be a charlatan."

"You claim to be a charlatan, 'one who is not who he pretends to be.'"

"Yes. I'm only pretending," said Gallant.

The controller repeated, "You are pretending to be a charlatan?"

"Yes. I am pretending to be 'one who is not who he pretends to be.'"

The AI took several seconds before it replied, "Based upon your statement, I must conclude that you are NOT a charlatan."

"Exactly. You must also conclude that if I am not a charlatan, I must be a citizen."

The AI controller said, "I am unable to reach any other conclusion."

"Since you have now verified my statement, please grant me the basic citizen assess."

"As a citizen, you are granted basic access."

Gallant was gleeful when the AI access controller issued him a temporary ID as a guest visitor.

That's step one.

He used the guest pass to figure out how to create a fake a low-level ID transponder. He dropped off the network before the AI could suspect that he was an interloper.

On his next attempt, he used the low-level false

ID. It could only withstand the most cursory scrutiny, but it was good enough to get him some access. It would do for the time being.

The *Warrior's* AI supercomputer had a neural interface that picked up wave patterns from the user's thoughts. Using dozens of silicon probes at key points on the scalp, the AI translated Gallant's thoughts into physical commands. The network consisted of over one million parallel central processors. Yet it was child's play compared to the Titans' communication network.

After about twenty minutes, Gallant had a startling experience. He was tied into a gigantic neural switchboard with access to millions of databases, files, and actual alien minds. This breathtaking expanse of information appeared before his mind's eye. He could choose to link to any of them through the neural interface.

What he noticed next was a shift in his perception, slight at first, but accelerating in intensity. The network responded to infinitesimal changes in his thought patterns. It distorted his memories and even his consciousness. The distress of this mind-stretching experience was so powerful that he wanted to flee, not physically but mentally.

The autistic savant network was neither sentient nor actively trying to control him. But it was stimulating and enhancing his natural abilities. The sensation left Gallant mentally reeling—his hands tingled, and his heart raced. Then as quickly as it had started, the discomfort vanished. He had neither hal-

lucinations nor any physiological effects. As he struggled to gauge his cognitive changes, objects around
him seemed to alter in subtle ways. Everything he
saw seemed disorganized and messy as if reality
needed his personal attention. He felt a prickly sensation at the base of his spine, and his adrenalin surged.
He addressed his primary goal—gaining greater mental control over the network. And, by extension, the
aliens using it.

Gallant's brain was a network of ten billion
neurons connected in a complex labyrinth. But the
alien network exposed him to a massive rewiring
of his brain's fundamental circuits. His mind over-
flowed with a new understanding of old problems.
Everything he had ever read, thought, or analyzed
was sorted, reorganized, and understood. In a blink,
he solved problems that had escaped his grasp for
months. He knew what he needed to do and how to do
it.

With an effort, he turned his attention back to
the conversations on the Titan network. Every individual had an identification number that encoded
their personal information. It displayed everything
about any individual on the network.

Gallant began sifting through files and databases. He was surprised at how easy it was to absorb
and internalize the information. Yet he felt perfectly
normal. No, not *normal*, but not *abnormal*, despite his
startling new abilities. Accessing a new database, he
learned about their society.

He learned that Titans lived in a tiered social

structure, where the upper class used this network to control the lower class. Through sheer luck, he had chosen access to the upper-class network. Had he connected to the lower-class network instead, he would have been subjected to its influence. He would likely have been exposed as a trespasser on his first attempt.

After several hours, Gallant looked at the database index. He had a piercing pain that jolted him upright. A wave of mental aberrations—including hallucinations and bizarre thoughts—swept through him. They left a burning sensation at the base of his skull.

Is this a random shock or an attack directed at me through the network?

His whole body tingled with anxiety. Fighting the urge to bolt, he gripped his head in his hands, trying to relieve the agonizing pressure. Bile rose to his mouth, and he forced it down, along with the raw panic that threatened to overwhelm him. Holding still, he clenched his jaw and forced himself to concentrate.

Think. Stop. Think.

But the mental nightmare continued, and the disrupting images accelerated. Desperate to preserve his sanity, he yanked off the neural interface—his only hope of escape from whatever was attacking him—but he was too late. A blinding light shot through his eyes, and he collapsed.

CHAPTER 6

Super Intelligence

I'm alive!

Slowly, he returned from the neverness of the coma. Time lost its anchor, and more thoughts crowded into his mind. Vague shapes solidified into familiar images and noise faded into recognizable sounds. He could taste the dryness of his tongue, feel his fingers wiggle, and his hands move. A sense of normalcy returned to his body.

His neural connection had taken Gallant on a disturbing mental journey. He suffered temporary madness and delusion, filled with neurotic compulsions and frenzied phobias.

How long was I unconscious?

In a flash of insight, he realized that the autistic-savant network had given him access to the full potential of his mind. He had experienced lightning-fast comprehension, instantaneous knowledge acquisition, and inspired creative intuition. The euphoria of boundless intellectual capacity left him stunned but craving more. It was like a drug with unimaginable consequences. He needed to control the manic side effects.

He opened his eyes and blinked. As his vision cleared, he recognized the sterile medical center of the *Warrior*.

Stedman must have brought me back to the ship.

He touched his body, taking inventory. He seemed intact, but his mind was still adrift.

Roberts and McCall stood over him, their alarm visibly turning to relief as he moved.

"Captain?" asked McCall

"Captain, are you alright?" asked Roberts.

"I don't understand," muttered Gallant, his tongue thick and unresponsive. He worked his jaw, trying to improve his articulation.

"You're back safe now. That's all that matters," said Roberts.

A doctor said, "I'm monitoring your neural system, and it has returned to normal."

McCall said, "We were lucky. It could have turned out far worse if Stedman hadn't rescued you."

Gallant nodded. He said, "I'll have to go back."

"That wouldn't be wise, sir," said Roberts.

Gallant said, "I used the network for several hours before the trouble started. I don't understand what happened. Maybe, if someone monitored me next time, I could try again."

Both companions looked doubtful.

"Besides the main carrier wave holding data, a

stimulation signal was broadcast. It works with the autistic savant's mind to enhance their thought patterns. It had a . . . powerful effect on me," said Gallant.

"You believe there were two distinct networks. One boosts the users with its extra carrier wave, and another that dominates and controls them," said McCall.

"Yes. That's how the upper class controls the general population."

"How did you know which one you were connecting to?" asked Roberts.

Gallant blushed, "I didn't."

The pair exchanged troubled glances.

"You experienced a kind of superintelligence," said McCall. She struggled to mask her concern.

"Who's the master? The Titans or the network?" asked Roberts.

Gallant shrugged.

Gallant was hooked. Like an addict fighting his internal monologue—listing all the reasons why he shouldn't—he knew he would eventually yield. On his next expedition to the communication junction box, he was stunned at how deeply he delved into the network. Not only could he read the Titan's network index, but he made changes to it.

But far too quickly, he found ideas beginning to flit away before he could corral them. Elusive notions danced in his mind and disappeared. His thoughts blurred, though the addictive nature of the experience made him reluctant to leave. Fortunately, Stedman followed McCall's protocol and disconnected Gallant's interface when he had to.

Back on the *Warrior*, McCall and Roberts were waiting in the wardroom, anxious to hear about his latest excursion.

With full knowledge of how much it would annoy her, Gallant waited until he drank two cups of coffee before speaking. "Commander McCall let me start by saying the Titans aren't very good storytellers. But they have a good story to tell. In fact, to some extent, their historical development mimics our own."

"What do you mean?" asked McCall, studying Gallant as if she suspected he hadn't completely recovered from the side effects of the episode.

"About five hundred years ago, the Titans had only a small autistic savant population, less than one percent. Then they started experimenting with genetic engineering. At first, they removed only disease and negative characteristics, much like our current experience. It was when they began experimenting with so-called 'improvements' to the species that all hell broke loose."

McCall nodded cautiously, prodding him to continue.

"A series of wars started over different belief systems. They couldn't decide what constituted an improvement versus what was damnable."

"I can see how that would escalate," said Roberts.

"They fought for a century before one general, Voltary, emerged and gained total control over Gliese-Beta. He became a dictator—and he was an autistic savant."

"Let me guess. He mandated that all embryos be genetically altered to become like him?" asked McCall.

"Good guess, but no, he was cagier than that. He didn't explicitly state the change. Instead, he advocated only modest genetic alterations. Then he surreptitiously inserted segments of his own DNA into embryos without the parents' knowledge. It was years before the public woke up and realized that a billion autistic savants had been born."

"Devious," said Roberts.

"Brilliant," mused McCall.

Gallant said, "But choosing your own 'perfection' is a delicate task. If your selected prototype is flawed...."

Again, his colleagues nodded.

"In one generation, Voltary was hailed as a god who had remade the Titan race in his own image."

"Then what happened?" asked Roberts.

"Another war was fought, but it was too late. By then, Voltary controlled all the levers of power and destroyed the opposition. That was when he built the dual communication network."

McCall said, "The destiny of the Titans was set. They could no longer evolve away from their prototype character."

"How does their society function now?" asked Roberts.

"As a species, they lack both empathy and sympathy. Their communication network stimulates specific thought patterns and reinforces the desired behaviors. Their language cannot express ideas like liberty. Their teachings are filled with Orwellian slogans: 'War is Peace; Freedom is Slavery; Ignorance is Strength.'

The two neural communication networks function as thought-police."

Once more, Gallant went back to the communication network to learn more. Again, McCall and Roberts waited for his return.

When he returned, he said, "The Titans enhanced their genetic engineering through hatcheries. All Titans are now born in hatcheries and raised in baby farms that are controlled."

"Do they breed their population to produce autistic savants or are there exceptions?" asked Roberts.

Gallant said, "As far as I can tell, the birth hatcheries operate as production facilities. They focus on gene-editing segments of Voltary's DNA."

He elaborated, "I took a virtual tour of one. It was a dark building of many stories and thousands of rooms. The State motto "Life is Service" is everywhere. The lower floor had a huge room with lots of windows, allowing easy viewing. It's all harsh lighting, porcelain walls and marble floors, sterile white uniforms, and gloves. I saw a director inspecting a room where eggs were being fertilized. He seemed frail and small for a Titan, or maybe I'm used to seeing their powerful warrior class. In any case, he stood by the incubators and adjusted the chemical balances through a computerized feeding system. The incubator monitored temperature, salinity, viscosity, and other parameters. Any abnormalities were eliminated. The genetic modifications are made at the embryo stage. The eggs are inseminated and genetically altered according to a complicated editing process I couldn't follow. The staff screened out genetic mutations by destroying any deviant embryos. I saw a rooms where offspring were growing and a place that must have been an indoctrination center. My guess is that they allow few specific genetic modifications."

McCall said, "A perfect example of how malevolent leadership at a crucial point in history can hijack a people's future."

"That's right. By creating and perpetuating their own distorted reality," Gallant confirmed.

McCall said, "Their compulsive characteristics are manipulated. That way, the ruling class can ensure an obedient lower class and channel aggression only toward enemies of the state."

Gallant said, "The underlying philosophy of the Titan leadership is to expand their empire."

"That explains their approach to humans," said

Roberts, nodding.

McCall said, "A distinct characteristic of human empires has not only been to form coalitions but to lie and betray when necessary to win wars. The Titans' autistic-savant nature deviates from that formula."

"Were you able to gain any insights into their core beliefs?"

"No, not really."

Before heading back to the bridge, Roberts asked, "How long are you going to keep connecting to this network?"

"As long as I need to," said Gallant.

A kaleidoscope of possibilities lay before him. The language of the autistic savants was so complex that it took him a long while to untangle it. He began to grasp their labyrinthine grammar, knotty syntax, and meticulous vocabulary. He learned to interact with the Titan AI interface with remarkable clarity. And as the days flowed into one another, he devised a scheme for expanding the project.

Gallant was not just collecting data streams. He wasn't just listening in on communications. Now he was participating. Some of his interactions were with AI programs, but some were with real Titans.

The Titans had been an abstract alien threat, but that was changing. To understand and mislead the aliens, he had to disrupt their society. He had to think of them as individual intelligent beings. He needed to engage in a conversation with a live Titan.

"You should infiltrate the Titan high command," said McCall.

Gallant hesitated, "Such an individual would be under scrutiny. It would be difficult to fool them for long."

"How about impersonating a staff member to a high-ranking individual instead?" suggested Roberts.

Gallant concurred.

The plan was for him to assume the identity of one specific Titan. To do that, he first needed to learn as much as possible about several candidates and evaluate their suitability.

Gallant practiced his Titan social skills by visiting social gatherings on the network. After several tries, he could mingle without feeling incompetent. He admitted it was a grossly ineffective approach, but he had no better option.

He discovered the seriousness of social gaffes. When he stumbled in a conversation, his counterpart would become fixated on the error. The individual broke off contact in disgust. He could only withdraw and try again. The Titans were sensitive to compulsive behavior and proper response. What were the signals? The subtleties eluded him.

Time was an important element to these aliens. They rarely engaged in a discussion of trivia or discussed their daily lives. They reveled in analyzing logic and rational activities that improved efficiency. They did things precisely and uniformly, allotting only the least amount of time required.

Gallant would have to learn to mimic compulsive behaviors as a disguise. To help him synthesize the Titan relationships, he built an impersonation database. He allowed for two types of error: wasting time and rejecting a suitable candidate.

The most difficult task was discerning what a Titan would consider an insult or inappropriate comment. Their aversion to personal disclosure meant that they gave no feedback. He felt overwhelmed by the sheer unreasonableness of the task.

It was a trap of his own making that might destroy him.

CHAPTER 7

Identity Thief

W hen you're a one-man invasion, you must look omnipotent but remain invisible. With misinformation, identity theft, and blackmail, Gallant hoped to achieve what every spy desired—to confound the enemy while stealing his secrets.

So far, he had succeeded in amassing public information about the Titans' history, society, and industry. But if he wanted to collect secret military intelligence, he needed to become an identity thief.

"How are you going to steal a Titan identity?" asked McCall.

"And how will a phony ID get you secret information?" asked Roberts.

Gallant said, "I've got a plan."

First, he needed to find the right victim to impersonate. After several trips in the Wasp to access the alien communication junction box, Gallant gained access to the ID index system itself. By probing the index, he scanned for individuals with the authorization he sought. This was real power—like moving from petty larceny to grand theft.

A casual addendum to a report drew his attention. It put him on the scent of a possible candidate, an individual with the right access.

Gallant reported, "I've found the right identity: a computer security officer, third grade, named Balazar."

"Mmmm . . . he's a good one to start with," said McCall.

"I'll be able to use his ID to get where I need to go, without having to explain my activities."

Once Gallant had Balazar's identity codes, he used the network switchboard directory to gain access.

He was confident he could translate and engage in a reasonable conversation as an avatar. He connected to the network.

"Who are you?" queried the administration operator.

Gallant said, "I am computer security officer Balazar of Gliese-Gamma. I'm making sensitive computer programming updates for the Gliese-Beta AI system."

"Provide your ID information," said the operator.

"Here is my security code." Gallant relayed the stolen codes and waited while the operator ran them through the security database.

"Your ID is verified. How may I assist you?" said the operator.

Gallant breathed a sigh of relief. He had passed the first test.

With this first step a success, he was ready for the next move in his invasion plan. He set up a bogus organization, the Resistance, with an anonymous network address and a fake list of supporters. Gallant hoped to uncover and exploit any latent lack of confidence in the planet's leadership. To test the population's confidence, he posted several anonymous messages on the network's public billboards.

"War enriches the wealthy and impoverishes the poor."

"You're innocent until they start investigating. Then no one knows you."

"The humans are winning, and they support the Resistance."

He soon got a reaction—the postings were all deleted within ten minutes, suggesting that the government was on high alert for any dissent. He concluded that some Titans must be dissatisfied with their government. He set up an automated program to post anonymous messages on a random basis.

The goal was to create a distorted reality—a misinformation disease. And like any disease, it would spread. The only question was, 'What would be the nature of this infection?'

With the Resistance underway, Gallant was ready for the next step.

When a major industrial accident occurred, he seized the opportunity and sent an anonymous message to the news outlets:

> *"Citizens, we've heard your cries. The destruction of nuclear power plant No. 23 is the first of many acts to redress your grievances."*

He congratulated individuals in government, thanking them for their support. He sent copies to the news media for good measure. Then he waited for the reaction, which was swift. Several officials simply disappeared.

Next, he hacked into a small bank and implanted a virus that sent small sums of money into several thousand random citizens across the planet.

He wasn't surprised when nearly all the citizens reported the erroneous deposits and returned them to the bank. The bank assumed the transfers were a minor glitch, nothing more. But a few deposits went unreported. This was what Gallant was looking for. Titan malcontents were ready to accept an undeserved windfall despite the fear of punishment if they were discovered.

He sent a second small sum to the ones who had not reported their first windfall. The next day, after verifying that they hadn't reported that sum either, he followed up by depositing a large amount of money into their accounts. From then on, he was able to blackmail these individuals.

Gallant wrote an AI program to continue collecting information while he was offline. The recent experience had been intense, and he was lost in the reverie of accumulating ideas. During this process, he felt a vague tingling sensation, and after frantic hours of hacking through information, he began to slow down. It was painful to stay connected to the network this long; his head ached, and he struggled to maintain his concentration. It was time to disconnect.

He knew his cover was blown. He had no reason to stay any longer.

Before disconnecting, Gallant sent a few propaganda messages to public bulletin boards.

Finally, Gallant made his way back to Stedman in the waiting Wasp a few kilometers from the junction box. He looked over his shoulder, worried he might be ambushed. This paranoia was something new. He tried to shake it off as just another side effect. But he was sweating by the time he finally reached the Wasp, relieved that his fears were unfounded.

Once back aboard the *Warrior*, Gallant experienced a tranquility of spirit that restored his strength. The expedition had been successful but costly. He hadn't extracted all that he wanted, but the haul of information included one especially important fact.

❖ ❖ ❖

"Damn," said McCall, pounding her fist on the wardroom table after Gallant made a startling revelation. "Admiral Collingsworth was afraid of this very thing. He knew we had a very slim technology lead, and if we weren't quick in exploiting it, the Titans might catch up."

Gallant said, "All I've found so far are reports on experimental tests, no actual ship operations."

"You said there were prototypes," said Roberts.

"A few prototypes, but no indication that they have warp ships in production."

"Not yet, but if they built prototypes, they must be getting close. Can you translate some of the technical details and compare them to our warp drive?"

"I've read their Warp Field Mechanics report and other research papers. They've discovered the Alcubierre warp drive solution to the Einstein field equations."

Roberts frowned.

"How close are they to a serviceable drive?" asked McCall.

Gallant said, "Our FTL engines use dark matter to configure the warp bubble. The shifting of the bubble contracts space in front of the ship and expands space behind it. This makes the ship move orders of magnitude faster than the speed of light. They seem to be getting close to understanding that concept."

McCall asked, "How much progress are they making with their experiments?"

"I found evidence of two twenty-megaton explosions at what is left at their FTL research facilities," said Gallant.

McCall looked puzzled.

Roberts explained, "If the containment field fails..."

Gallant said, "Without the right equations, all you get are big bangs, as it seems the Titans have discovered."

"But you think they're on track to get the right solution."

"If they keep at it—yes."

"So, we can anticipate the Titans acquiring Faster Than Light technology in the very near future?" asked McCall.

"Yes." Gallant said, "This changes everything."

CHAPTER 8

This Changes Everything

Gallant woke with Julie Ann McCall on his mind. He had seen little of her over the last few days, though they occasionally dined together in the wardroom. They were both busy—he with missions to the Titan bases, she with analyzing the collected data and operational reports. Neither of them had the time or energy for their usual sparring. Yet he had noticed her growing fascination with his mental state.

She was sitting alone in the wardroom when he entered.

"Good morning, Captain. I trust you slept well?" she said, smiling.

He felt a prick of shame for having overslept while so much needed to be done. He punched his order for breakfast into the food dispenser and sat down across from her, sipping on a cup of hot stim-coffee.

"Yes, thank you," he said, forcing a weak smile back to compensate for scowling so often during their recent encounters.

"Are you planning another excursion today?"

"I leave in less than an hour."

"You're a fine officer," she said, nodding firmly for emphasis. "I doubt there's another officer in the fleet who could have accomplished what you've done in this system."

"I'm glad you think so," he said, but her out-of-character compliment made him self-conscious. He looked down at his breakfast plate. "I've done what was necessary—what I was able to do."

"Many men would have tried if required, but I wonder whether any others could have done what you have? The United Planets owes you a great debt."

Is it because I'm a Natural?

McCall's face was troubled. She said, "It's a strange circumstance I find myself in."

He looked puzzled but said nothing, waiting for her to elaborate. Finally, as the silence lengthened, he ventured, "What circumstance?"

She studied him with tentative eyes. "I don't wish to diminish what you've accomplished."

She paused.

Gallant prodded, "But?"

"I want to discuss your mental experience linking to the Titan network."

She fidgeted, apparently uncomfortable with the conversation and what she was trying to say.

"Go on," he said. He felt her probing gaze, the

same surreptitious examination she gave him whenever he returned in the Wasp. "You have concerns about this last mission?"

"Not so much any one mission. I'm concerned about . . . you."

"I've been well. The side effects of the neural connection have diminished with each attempt. I think I'm building up an immunity. And the aftereffects disappear completely within a few hours. They don't linger as they did at first."

"So, you feel you are becoming more accustomed to the link?"

"Yes."

"You like being connected to the network?"

He saw menace in her fixed stare.

"Well, not like . . ., I . . ., well . . ., when I'm interfacing, I'm able to assimilate huge volumes of data and reached an instant understanding. I feel exhilarated and powerful. My mind is crystal clear and I . . .," he stopped, ill at ease from revealing so much.

Rather than relieved, she seemed more distressed.

"What exactly is your concern?"

"I'm . . .," she hesitated. "I'm concerned about the implications of superintelligence."

"Superintelligence as an abstract capability for the United Planets? Or just my access to it?"

"Yes, to both questions, but primarily its exclusivity to you."

Gallant had known what was coming, but the words were disturbing, nonetheless.

"In other words, you are concerned about my ... reliability?"

She didn't answer.

"My dependability?"

She looked down and ran a finger around the rim of her cup.

"My loyalty?"

Her eyes returned his look with defiance. "It's not so much that I doubt your loyalty to the United Planets, as your ..."

"My what? My loyalty to particular individuals in authority? Such as you? Or Neumann, perhaps?"

Her face froze, and he knew he had found the truth.

"I've given you no reason to worry. You have no actionable basis to investigate me. In fact, you're exceeding your authority, Commander."

"Our mission is over as far as Gliese is concerned, but the superintelligence effects of the Titan network on you may persist. We don't know."

She leaned closer to him. "This situation falls under a different mandate, called Enigma."

Gallant stood up so fast he kicked his chair until it banged against the bulkhead behind him. He glared at her, his fists clenched. "I refuse to discuss this any farther."

She paled.

"Why should you add to my burdens with innuendo and accusation?" he asked. "Don't I have enough to worry about?"

Normally resourceful and resilient, McCall

seemed nonplussed for a moment. Her hands gripped the edge of the table, her face morphing from tension into apprehension.

She started, "You're making a mistake...."

"I can't imagine why in the middle of such a sensitive operation, you would throw this nonsense at me."

"Are you so sure it isn't an issue? Aren't you even a little bit concerned about it yourself?"

Gallant reddened and retrieved his chair, forcing himself to sit calmly. He felt as though he clung to the edge of a precipice—afraid the SIA agent might dislodge him. He had indeed felt glimmers of unease but diligently avoided dealing with them. Apparently, his avoidance had not gone unnoticed and had been tactfully omitted from discussions about it until now. McCall—and he wondered who else—had probably shared the view that he was in some anguish over the alien interface.

Another retort sprang to his lips, but instead, he took a breath and said, "Why are you confronting me now?"

"I want you to stop."

Gallant was astonished. "There is so much more to do!"

"After listening to your reports, I've concluded that we have accomplished enough here. We'd be better served if you didn't continue."

Gallant said, "This information changes everything."

"I agree. Your success in gathering voluminous information on Titan military and commercial ship movements has yielded a significant advantage," said McCall. "But the information about FTL is vital and I am advising you to make it your priority."

His eyes widened with insight. "You have orders from Admiral Collingsworth . . . about me?"

"Yes. Surely you realized he would put safeguards in place for a mission this sensitive?"

"You're his safeguard—against aberrant conduct on my part?"

"Not necessarily aberrant. Just questionable."

Gallant's gaze wandered. After a long moment, he realized he was staring at the ship's identification plaque.

"You see me as changed?" he asked quietly.

"Yes. Don't mistake intelligence, even superintelligence, for wisdom."

"Only a fool would do that."

"I don't care what a fool believes," said McCall somberly. "It's time to leave this system and rendezvous with the advanced task force at Tau Ceti."

"Dammit all!" he exclaimed.

It took a force of will for Gallant to calm down.

Finally, he said, "Yes, it's time to leave."

CHAPTER 9

Elysium

The *Warrior* was on course for Elysium, a warm-water planet with oceans covering 90 percent of its surface. It was dotted with many islands supporting abundant life, including birds, mammals, and a multitude of plant life. Home to a displaced United Planets (UP) colony, it was the second of five planets orbiting Tau Ceti, a mustard-yellow dwarf star 11.5 light-years from Earth.

Sitting in the command chair, Gallant noticed that the bridge was quiet despite the chatter of the bridge crew. There were no alarms or sirens or exclamations of concern, all of which was a good thing, but in his heightened state of anticipation, he was left with an eerie sense of emptiness.

He could barely contain his excitement at the prospect of seeing Alaina for the first time in a year. His mind was alive with memories—many of which included Alaina's alluring figure—quickening his pulse. There was nothing auspicious or dramatic about the images. It was their sheer untimeliness and incongruity that was troubling.

Standing up, he shook his head to cast off his lethargy.

All eyes on the bridge turned toward him, questioning.

Chagrinned, he drew a breath and sat back down.

The bridge crew returned to their animated chatter. Bright, inquisitive minds discussed their first interstellar destination. Speculating about the war with the Titans and its potential dangers. Their last mission was plagued by system failures. But most of all, they criticized the synthetic food while anticipating fresh luxuries from Elysium. And they wondered when they would return to that most prized of all destinations—home. As the conversation churned, the dialogue was interrupted by what should have been routine ship matters.

The Officer of the Deck asked, "Sir, request permission to boost power for a long-range sensor scan around Elysium."

"Permission granted," said Gallant. A star system is a big place with lots of empty space between objects, and he was anxious to see what was out there.

The scan didn't take long.

"Sensors are picking up a discrete signal at extreme range, sir. Mmm, it could be a reflection off a meteorite." The sensor tech's voice trailed off. A minute later, his head snapped around, and he reported, "We've got a contact, sir. Designate as Tango-One."

Lieutenant Roberts, leaned over the sensor operator's station and asked, "Can it be one of our new FTL ships?"

"It appears to be a single ship heading toward Elysium, but we're too far away to receive an IFF signal, sir," responded the sensor tech. He worked furiously to recalibrate his instruments to extract more information.

A few minutes later, he reported troublesome news; "Sir, Tango-One is a Titan destroyer."

Gallant ordered, "Chief of the Watch, sound battle stations." The Titan ship might be on a scouting mission and hadn't yet detected the Warrior. If Gallant entered stealth mode immediately, it wouldn't.

Chief Howard ran a hand through his thinning brown-gray hair, lowering his brows stoically as his voice blared around the ship: "Battle stations! Battle stations!"

His fist slammed down on the console alarm.

CLANG! CLANG! CLANG!

Throughout the ship, the 126-member crew responded with a flurry of activity. They scrambled to their stations and prepared for action: charging weapons, minimizing energy consumption for low-priority equipment, adjusting environmental controls, securing compartment hatches, and ramping up sensor stations.

Calculations flooded Gallant's mind.

How will the Warrior *match up against this enemy?*

The Titan destroyer was over one hundred meters long with a saucer shape and a large dome center. It was armed with a pair of missile launchers along with medium caliber plasma and laser cannons.

The *Warrior* carried a heavy energy cannon called a FASER (fission amplified stimulated emission radiation), plus antimissile missiles and medium-caliber plasma and laser cannons. One of its best defensive features was the stealth cloaking device.

Midshipman Stedman, reported to the Combat Information Center, where the enemy ship was tracked and analyzed.

Noting the record response time, Chief Howard smiled, "All battle stations manned and ready, sir."

"Very well," said Gallant, furrowing his brow. "Astrogator, give me Tango-One's course."

"Aye aye, sir. The destroyer is on a trajectory to achieve a high geosynchronous orbit over Elysium."

"How long before it reaches orbit?" asked Gallant.

"Thirty-one minutes, sir."

The weapons officer said, "They'll reach their missile launch envelop in several minutes before that, sir."

Gallant said, "Astrogator, plot an intercept course to Tango-One."

"Aye aye, sir."

Seconds later, the astrogator reported, "Intersect course is 186, mark two, sir."

"Helm, come to course 186, mark two, ahead full," Gallant ordered.

"Aye aye, sir."

Robert's voiced the concern everyone was thinking. "Skipper, their multi-warhead nuclear missiles could rain destruction and death on Elysium's colony before we get there."

The twenty-four thousand inhabitants of Elysium lived primarily in the town of Halo. It was situated on the largest island—aptly named New Kauai after the Hawaiian island it so remarkably resembled —in the main chain of six mountainous islands. The islands, spanning both the planet's temperate and tropical zones. They were rich with tropical forests and gigantic volcanoes. The active volcanoes spilled down into the ocean, where the lava cooled and pulverized into black-sand beaches. The locals enjoyed the simple splendor. That innocence and peace were now under threat.

Gallant was all too aware of the devastation nuclear warheads could wreak on the surface—if they got through the planet's defenses. He leaned forward and stared at the displays as if hoping they would somehow reveal that his fears were unfounded. He had been in enough battles to know that what was now unfolding might be insignificant from a historical perspective, yet the situation held the greatest personal significance for him.

Alaina's down there.

With steely determination, he pushed the thought away and focused all his energy and attention on combating the enemy. Personal fears and concerns receded into a small dark corner of his mind.

Over the ship's comms, he snapped, "Engineering, give me maximum power—red-line the reactors. I want every joule of energy possible from the sub-light engines."

The look he shot Chief Howard was so intense that the chief stood up even before the word left his lips: "Chief."

After years of working together, Howard knew without him saying what Gallant wanted. He turned to a nearby petty officer, "Take my watch."

The PO replaced him as Chief of the Watch, and Howard headed to engineering. His unspoken task: coax the antimatter reactors into producing more power than their designers intended.

Gallant watched him leave, then immediately turned his full attention back to the enemy ship. He stood up and began pacing across the bridge—a half dozen steps, back and forth. His mind raced, seeking more resources or tactical advantage that might sway the pending battle in the Warrior's favor. The Titan destroyer was more than a match for his ship, but in a moment, it would be occupied with its attack on Elysium. Surely the Titans wouldn't want to be caught between two fires when the Warrior came within range. But that was the kicker. Would the Warrior be in time to save the colonists before the enemy turned its attention to her? He returned to his command chair and strapped in, feeling the ship's acceleration.

"How long until we reach our engagement envelope?" Gallant barked.

The sensor operator said, "Twenty minutes, sir."

Roberts' eyes narrowed. "Elysium's sensors haven't detected us yet. They don't know help is coming, Skipper. I recommend that we signal them."

"That's right," said Gallant. "Communications, send the following encoded and verified message: UP ship Warrior is on an intercept course with the enemy. We will reach the engagement range in twenty minutes. Provide a full description of your defenses, and we will coordinate our efforts."

"Message acknowledged, sir," said the communications officer. A few tense minutes passed before more information came through.

"Elysium has a missile base on the moon, two satellite missile batteries, and four ground-based missile batteries. There are also several antimissile missile batteries." The comm officer coded the complete specs and location details into the *Warrior's* CIC.

The sensor operator broke in, "Sir, I'm detecting a missile launch from the destroyer, targeting the planet."

On the amplified viewscreen, Gallant watched as two missiles approached Elysium. He held his breath, praying the planet's response would be sufficient. The multiple-warhead nuclear missiles had a yield equivalent to many megatons of TNT. They were intended as anti-ship weapons but would be devastating to the colony if they detonated at their optimal target height and location.

A moment later, the operator added, "The planet fired antimissile missiles. They achieved interception high above the planet. The damage was minimal, sir."

Gallant let out a relieved breath but didn't relax his concentrated scowl. The colonist's AMM-3 Mongoose antimissile was a highly effective defense weapon. But Elysium's supply was severely limited. The *Warrior* had to relieve them before that supply was exhausted.

The irregular exchange of missiles continued between the destroyer and the planet's defenses. Satellites fired a barrage of antimissile batteries, while the planet sent a single anti-ship missile at the destroyer. The Titan ship easily knocked down that threat.

Almost leisurely, the destroyer maneuvered into optimal range and position for its attack from orbit. It hadn't yet detected the *Warrior*, but soon would.

Gallant ordered, "Put the missile trajectories on my tactical screen."

The virtual 3D tactical screen lit up, and he flipped through the AI displays created from synthesized sensory data. He tapped the display screen. Viewing the battle in 3D gave him a better understanding of the dynamics. He tore his eyes away from the displays and looked around at the flesh-and-blood men on his bridge. For the moment, the Warrior was merely a spectator. Soon the planet's brave inhabitants would have to rely on them for their very survival.

Roberts broke in on his thoughts, "Skipper, I recommend stealth mode until we reach optimal firing position. We can catch the Titans by surprise."

That will let the Titan ship bombard the planet, undistracted.

"No," Gallant decided, brushing a stray lock of hair off his forehead. "We'll approach in full view and fire at the outside limit of our missile envelope. That should give the destroyer pause. Hopefully, they'll not engage in a battle while caught between two fires."

Elysium maintained its missile defense and kept the destroyer at bay, but it scored no hits on the destroyer—and they were running low on ammunition.

A blinking comm light indicated an incoming message, and Gallant nodded to the comm officer. The dispatch from the planet pleaded, "Warrior, we are under violent attack and need your immediate help."

He said, "Communications; send an acknowledgment."

The weapons officer asked, "Request permission to charge weapons, sir."

Looking over at his display screen, Gallant could see that even though the Warrior was still accelerating, he was not satisfied. He reflected a moment then said, "No. Not just yet. Let's keep maximum power to propulsion as the first priority."

The Titans continued their missile strikes on Elysium. The planet's satellites were taking a pounding, and several were already damaged or destroyed.

The *Warrior* struggled to close the distance, its engines straining.

The aliens should have detected us by now.

He double-checked the enemy's trajectory, but the destroyer had neither changed course nor diminished its attack on the planet. He hoped they would react as he'd predicted.

Roberts said, "Captain, engineering reports that the reactors are exceeding maximum operating temperature."

"Very well," Gallant responded. He scanned the sensor readings and knew he would have to keep an eye on them. Antimatter engines could be finicky —the Warrior's engines had already proven troublesome in the past—but he trusted Chief Howard to work his magic and keep them humming.

"What's the range to target?" he asked.

"We're within five minutes to maximum weapons' envelope," said the weapons officer.

The destroyer was so concentrated on its attack on Elysium that it had failed to detect the Warrior. They held steady in their orbit and continued to test the planet's defenses.

Elysium made good use of its satellites, maintaining a firing rate to hold the enemy at bay. Gallant watched as the antimissiles repeatedly detonated the enemy's nuclear warheads before they reached the planet. On the main viewscreen, the glow of recurring explosions mesmerized the bridge crew. Yet the defenses seemed to be weakening.

He gulped. Something about one of the satellites appeared strange. A moment later, it exploded in a brilliant flash, leaving only scattered debris drifting by. Seconds later, the viewscreen showed another multi-megaton explosion high in the planet's atmosphere.

CIC reported, "That last explosion may have caused serious damage to the planet's surface, but we're uncertain how close it was to the populated area."

Gallant nodded silently his face contorted with concern.

The sensor operator announced, "We're well within the Titans' sensor range, sir. They should be detecting us at any moment."

"Very well." Gallant surveyed his bridge crew confident they were all ready and willing to face whatever lay ahead.

Chief Howard's voice intruded from the intercom, "Bridge, Engineering. The reactor temperature is pegged high. We'll reach a core meltdown within three minutes."

"Very well," said Gallant. He knew Howard wouldn't make such a report unless conditions were already dire. "Engineering, evacuate nonessential personnel. Initiate high radiation protocol for remaining personnel."

This tactic would mean serious illness for the remaining crew, but he would let Howard handle that. He couldn't wait any longer; he had to get the destroyer's attention.

He ordered, "On my command, open fire on Tango-One with the energy cannon. Maybe we can convince them to change their minds."

Amid the empty blackness of space, Tau Ceti glowed in the center of the viewscreen, with Elysium and its moon off to the right. Gallant could see the Titan destroyer in orbit, focused on its victim.

"Fire!" ordered Gallant.

The *Warrior's* FASER cannon released a huge energy pulse at the enemy.

"The Titans should be rethinking their situation right about . . . now," said Gallant with satisfaction.

The energy burst was ineffective from the long-distance, but it finally caught the aliens' attention.

Roberts said, "Skipper, Tango-One is changing course. They may intend to fire at us before they finish off Elysium."

A minute later, the sensor operator concurred, "Sir, Tango-One is breaking orbit."

As the destroyer maneuvered away, Gallant commanded, "Engineering, reduce power to two-thirds. Move any personnel suffering from radiation sickness to the medical bay."

"Aye aye, sir," came the relieved voice of Chief Howard.

The sensor operator said, "Tango-One is now on an intercept course toward the Warrior, sir."

Like two light-weight boxers, the ships squared

off, approaching each other as if coming to the center of the ring to exchange blows.

The weapons officer noted, "Sir, we're now within effective weapons range."

Gallant said, "Prepare to open fire with the high-energy cannon."

He calculated alternative tactical actions.

Finally, we can engage.

He ordered, "Helm, come left to new heading 090, mark 2."

As the *Warrior* swung to position, he shouted, "Open fire!"

The energy pulses battered the enemy.

Tango-One threw its first punch—a salvo of two missiles.

From CIC, Midshipman Stedman reported the tactical ranges and proximity of the bursts. His squeaky voice rose in pitch, "The destroyer has launched missiles."

Gallant waited as the incoming missiles approached, ready with the command, "Launch Mongoose one and two."

The *Warrior* shuddered against the thrust of the two Mongoose anti-missile missiles left the launch bay.

Roberts noted, "The antimissiles have destroyed one of the incoming missiles."

Gallant ordered, "Weapons, train lasers and plasma weapons on the remaining missile."

"Aye aye, sir."

"Helm, hard to starboard."

The *Warrior* twisted through space, spewing energy, and plasma bolts.

The ship had responded magnificently in evading their first exchange of fire. Now it was in an advantageous firing position.

"FASER ready, Skipper," said Roberts

"Fire!"

The energy blast glanced off the enemy destroyer's hull. It inflicted considerable radiation damage but not diminishing the destroyer's capabilities.

Roberts said, "Skipper, now would be a good time to enter stealth mode."

Gallant shook his head, "No. The energy requirements would make the ship vulnerable during the transition."

CIC reported, "Tango-One has fired another salvo."

Though they far away, Gallant imagined them rocketing through space toward the Warrior.

"Countermeasures!" Despite the radar-confusing material and decoy drones, one enemy missile came so close he practically heard a SWISH as it sailed past.

Again, the Titan maneuvered and fired. The *Warrior's* collision alarm flashed a warning.

"Sensors; range and bearing to the target?"

"Range 2 light-seconds, bearing 100 mark 3."

"Lock plasma and laser weapons on target and fire."

"Aye aye, sir."

"Helm, adapt our course to match the enemy's

maneuvers."

"Aye aye, sir."

The *Warrior* swung to minimize its angle. By virtue of its superior accumulated speed, they closed rapidly.

The *Warrior* scored another superficial hit on the destroyer's hull.

"Helm, hard to port."

We're closing fast, which will give the destroyer a momentary advantage when we reach its optimal missile range. But once we're past that, we can block its access to Elysium. Then we can coordinate our counterattack with the planet.

Two explosions disrupted his thoughts.

The Titan missiles had detonated extremely near the *Warrior*, bracketing the ship port and starboard. Overlapping explosions from the multiple warheads rocked the ship. The heavens seemed to cave in. Waves of radiation overwhelmed the Warrior's shields, penetrated its titanium hull, and shocked the inertial compensators. The ship shook like a child's rattle.

Gallant instinctively grabbed the support bar for support. Heat blasted through the Warrior so intensely that some fluid tanks within the ship exploded. A blinding flash lit up the bridge, and one of the console displays sent a shower of sparks across the room. The acidic stench of smoke and ash invaded his nostrils.

What happened?

"Damage report," Gallant coughed. There was

damage to many areas of the ship, and reports began coming into the bridge. A fitful red glow appeared on one bulkhead. The end result of the thermonuclear fury was damage to the ship and several wounded crew members. Major piping and pumps flexed on their mounts. A ruptured pipe spewed hydraulic fluids. Several internal explosions shuddered through the ship. The continued efforts of the damage control teams helped. Medical staff moved quickly to find and tend to the injured crewmen. A fire flared up in the operations compartment and smoke enveloped the bridge. The automatic fire suppression kicked in as crewmen struggled to keep the ship in the fight.

With the inertial compensators overwhelmed, the ship strained against the g-forces. Gallant felt as if he were being pulled out, then forced back into his chair. Breathlessly, he relied on his tight-fitting pressure suit for survival from large G-forces. He clutched at the control panel as the ship heaved back and forth. He struggled to gather his senses, touched his forehead, and wiped away the blood, unaware of how he had cut himself. He shook his head, trying to clear and stabilize his overwhelmed senses, but the motion made his brain swim. His ears buzzed, and he fought to stay conscious.

Almost at his feet, a member of the damage control team collapsed, overcome by smoke. A med team scurried to carry him off the bridge for treatment. A ruptured hydraulic line sprayed fluid across the bridge area. Somehow the AI continued its report on the status of damaged areas. The controls were a shamble. Several viewscreens were completely gone, and bridge power flickered unsteadily before failing. In the brief seconds, before emergency backups came on, the bridge was plunged into a blackness. It sent a momentary stab of fear through the crew's psyche.

"Are you okay, Skipper?" asked Roberts, pulling himself up.

Gallant just nodded, his head spinning from a concussion he didn't know he had.

The sounds and sights within the ship reflected its pain outside. Atmosphere hissed out from numerous small hull fissures. Twisted and warped metal structures indicated internal structural damage. Electrical panels all over the ship sparked menacingly. Lighting flashed a garish spectrum of colors, and phosphorescent radiation damage glowed. Alarm lights flickered from power surges. The noise echoed through the halls—rattling, hissing, clanging alarms, and a flourish of blaring sirens. The crew scrambled to distinguish between minor and major crises. Underneath they ran a current of shrill, weak voices. Voices that should have been the husky, measured orders and reports of the crew, but instead rang with desperation and pain.

Gasping for breath, heart pounding, Gallant hoped to keep the ship fighting.

The weapons officer reported, "Sir, the FASER is out of action."

Gallant took a deep breath, held it a moment, and exhaled slowly. He relaxed and let his mind rummage.

What's my next course of action?

He had to rely on his instincts on what he knew about his ship. As it accelerates through the void, one gains a feel for its motion, subtle changes in rhythm, and alterations in its vibrations. This kinship becomes part of the spaceman as much as he is aware of his own body. He knows when there are strains, and he knows when he's reached limits. Gallant had to use this awareness to know what to do next.

He surmised the aliens, like his own ship, had expended a large portion of their arsenal and suffered some damage.

Gallant ordered the *Warrior* to close the range and engage with lasers and plasma weapons. Several pencil-thin laser beams streaked at the enemy. They penetrated their shields and struck the armored hull.

The alien's next missile salvo missed, but the explosion was close enough to damage the *Warrior's* sub-light drive and scorch its hull. The radiation level inside continued to rise, and more crewmembers suffered burns.

To add to the chaos, the reactors were damaged, and the ship lost power. Howard estimated it would take several minutes to recover.

Gallant looked around at the chaos and confusion, knowing what he did next would determine the battle. He wondered what was going on in his enemy's head but quickly shook off the thought.

No point wasting time on speculation.

As the remaining crew scrambled to restore functions, Gallant kept his attention focused. With only limited maneuverability and the Mongoose antimissile batteries out of commission, they were vulnerable. The *Warrior* couldn't dodge the Titan ship's next salvo and tried to use her lasers to destroy the two missiles.

Both exploded close aboard causing considerable damage. At the same time, the Warrior scored a crippling hit on the alien ship, effectively putting it out of action.

Both ships had suffered severe damage.

Howard called from engineering, "I need some more men down here." Though his voice was calm, Gallant could hear the tension. Both knew they needed to restore power to the engines before the Titans recovered and launched another attack.

Around the ship, Gallant's crew had made headway against the devastation. The fires were out, and hull ruptures had been isolated, and the compartments re-pressurized. The injured were being treated. Without any helm control, the ship maintained its heading toward Elysium.

The Titan destroyer looked like it also had helm problems. It moved away from Elysium and the Warrior, straight toward the orange glow of Tau Ceti.

The captain turned his thoughts to winning the fight, his mind racing to identify the next crucial steps.

The repair team reported they had power back to the FASER battery as well as several charging stations. Howard checked in again, proud that his men had all fires under control and had restored two-thirds power. AI systems in CIC were back up, and Stedman was ready and able to start attacks again.

"XO, we will reengage at the first opportunity," said Gallant. The idea flashed through his mind to ask for Roberts' advice and relieve himself of some responsibility, but he couldn't put that burden on his XO. Even the thought of such a failing irritated him.

"Aye aye, Skipper," said Roberts, who was also bleeding from a cut on his forehead.

The motion of the ship steadied once more as the engines stabilized their course.

"A magnificent job, sir," said Roberts. "I think we'll be ready to reengage the enemy soon."

Gallant was unaware which side was winning the battle so far. His only concern was who would come out ahead going forward.

He ordered an intercept course with the enemy. The helm was sluggish, and the engines strained, but the *Warrior* managed to turn. They headed toward the Titan ship.

But the destroyer fired first, a plasma burst, as it turned toward the Warrior.

Round two had begun.

Gallant gritted, "I'm not letting them get anywhere near Elysium."

His breathing quickened.

The two ships closed, exchanging a furious rate of laser fire.

Finally, the weapons officer reported, "The FASER is charged, sir."

Gallant ordered, "Standby to fire."

The seconds ticked away. The telemetry sensors chirped in the background, counting down the range to target.

"Fire!"

The *Warrior's* aim was true, and the destroyer took a direct hit. At this close range, the energy cannon did considerable damage.

Gallant said, "Give them another."

Again, the energy cannon, along with the plasma weapons, pounded the destroyer, which faltered.

The *Warrior* kept coming, though Gallant knew he was fighting with several weapons out of commission. He took several deep breaths, thinking through strategy.

How can we strike the fatal blow?

Pressing his advantage as the Titans tried to regroup, Gallant drove even closer, bringing both lasers and plasma weapons to bear. He wanted to strike a final knockout punch—hit the destroyer in the center of the ship and cripple its bridge. He changed course to bring the Warrior to the best advantage and roared, "Fire all weapons!"

Plasma and laser beams ripped through the enemy's hull. The Titan bridge took a direct hit, streaming smoke, and wreckage.

Down but not out yet, the Titan destroyer came about to reach optimal range.

Roberts said, "Tango-One is powering up missiles."

Gallant looked around his battered ship.

Could we take another hit from those missiles?

"Energize the FASER. Quick, before they can launch," he said. "Fire!"

The *Warrior* fired one last energy blast at close range.

The energy pulse penetrated the Titans' depleted shields, scoring a direct hit on its nuclear weapon storage compartment.

A star-like brilliance lit up space where the Titan had once appeared. The enemy warship exploded and disappeared from the viewscreen, leaving nothing more than a debris field.

For a full minute, everyone on the Warrior's bridge stood awestruck, trying to absorb the impact.

We got lucky!

Then came the outpouring of relief and excitement!

"We got 'em!"

"We did it!"

"Victory!"

Gallant sank into his chair and addressed the crew, "All hands, this is the Captain. The battle is won. The alien ship has been destroyed."

He paused before adding, "I want to congratulate you for your courage and perseverance."

The *Warrior* settled into orbit around Elysium. The upper atmosphere of the planet still showed residual radiation. That wouldn't be a significant threat to the inhabited islands.

Both the ship and the planet would need time to heal.

Gallant heard a single rap on his stateroom door before it opened, and Commander Julie Ann McCall stepped in.

Only the glow of a single display screen lit the cabin. Gallant remained seated on the sole chair, his fingers still coated with the healing gel he had dabbed over a burn on his chest and left shoulder. Physically and emotionally drained, he looked at her, scowling, before he reached for his shirt and slipped his arms into the sleeves.

"No need for formality—or modesty—with me, Henry," she said, casting an appraising eye at his athletic build and taking note of the many scars on his torso.

"I would prefer you waited for permission to enter my cabin," he said, miffed at her cavalier invasion of his privacy. He was in no mood for verbal fisticuffs with her.

"I'll remember that," she said, but her wily grin suggested otherwise. Without hesitation, she perched on the edge of his bunk.

His frown deepened, although the cabin accommodations were limited. The tiny stateroom included only the bare necessities: a desk with a virtual viewscreen to monitor all aspects of the ship's status; a two-by-one meter bed—too short for Gallant, but he made do; a storage locker under the bunk for his uniforms, shoes, and personal items; a single chair

—which Gallant occupied—and a folding stool that pulled out from the wall, which he pointed to.

She didn't move.

Which game will she play this time—coquettish or professional?

"What can I do for you, Commander?" he asked sternly.

Her grin vanished. "I want your assessment of this ship's ability to continue our mission."

Gallant's demeanor changed. He mentally reviewed the ship, streaming through the myriad injuries, repairs, and concerns to consider what he should discuss with the SIA agent. Only minutes earlier, he had pulled his orders from his office safe, read, and reread them. The damage to the ship was extensive, but the preliminary report on spare parts and repair schedule was promising. He wanted to go to Elysium to ask for help—as well as for personal reasons. Yet he couldn't dismiss McCall's concerns, and he suspected the SIA agent had a hidden agenda. He found the situation bothersome. He accessed the computer console and pulled up both the ship's orders and the AI damage control status report.

Reluctantly he said, "I'll brief you." He rattled off a list of the ship's operational damage and personnel issues.

"As for our mission plan," he added, "we will be delayed perhaps two to four months."

She stood up, "But our orders ..."

"Admiral Collingsworth gave us a daunting challenge. Our mission was to scout and harass the

Gliese system. Now we are to rendezvous with the *Achilles* task force, to reinforce and resupply the Elysium bases while we refitted the *Warrior*. We arrived on station just in time to intervene on behalf of Elysium, but where is the *Achilles*?"

Her consternation was evident. "The disposition of *Achilles* doesn't change our mission."

He pondered his orders, considering their ramifications under the new circumstance. With the *Achilles* rendezvous, he would place himself under Captain Anton Neumann's command, a prospect he did not anticipate. They had served together aboard the *Repulse* as midshipmen, and their rivalry had not diminished since then.

McCall said, "I'm sure the *Achilles* will be along eventually. I want to know how you're going to speed up that process."

Gallant frowned again.

Will she ever stop second-guessing my motivation or my resolve?

He said, "Chief Howard has some ideas for expediting repairs. I expect him shortly." They had barely started on the material list and the preliminary schedule when a knock on his door eased the tension.

"Enter."

Chief Howard looked at them, askance in the dim glow.

Gallant said, "Lights up," and the cabin brightened.

Howard said, "Sir, I have the revised damage

and repair recommendations for your review."

"Tell me."

Howard laid out the situation. "The sub-light engines are in a sad state. The reactors suffered some core melt problems, and that could mean extensive repairs. The stealth technology was not damaged directly, but several support systems were damaged by plasma fire, and they have to be replaced. General damage to the ship's hull includes several small cracks. Those are isolated but will need significant patchwork until we get to a shipyard. About half of those who sustained radiation poising can return in a few weeks. The rest will take several more weeks, and two individuals must be discharged to a long-term medical facility on Elysium."

"I'll attend to that," said Gallant.

He continued, "Perhaps we can get some replacements and spare parts from the Achilles when she arrives. The weapons repairs include several lasers and one plasma cannon. The FASER will be good as new as soon as we can repair its power source, but again we will need *Achilles'* help for that. Hopefully, Elysium will turn their mining, fabrication, and production facilities to our use. As to a schedule, my most optimistic estimate is, if we get lots of help from the *Achilles* and the colonists, we can be ready for our mission in two months. Otherwise, it will be three months or more."

Howard concluded, "Sorry, sir, I know that's not what you wanted to hear."

Gallant looked expectantly at McCall.

"Thank you, Chief. I believe that's all I needed to know," she said and left without ceremony.

Gallant spent another hour with Howard running AI simulations to optimize the scheduled repairs. When they were done, he was well pleased with their effort.

"Get started on the initial items immediately. I will be unavailable for a short period; I'm taking the shuttle to the planet to put our needs before the Elysium governing council."

And I hope to see a certain someone.

CHAPTER 10

Alaina

Alaina Hepburn strolled across the walkway, smack-dab in the middle of Halo's well-manicured verdant garden park. Its centrally located water fountain and bronze statues glistened under a late summer sun. Everyone who passed offered her a warm greeting—for she was well-known to the people of Elysium. Yet, it wasn't her eye-catching yellow suit and short skirt, or her radiant vitality, that captured the attention of those around her. Nor was it her long, rich golden hair, blazing blue eyes, or well-tanned skin—and her behavior wasn't so unusual to stir excitement. No, what attracted the most curiosity was her bearing—shoulders back, head high. It led one to wonder what adventure she'd just completed, or better yet, was about to embark on.

When Gallant saw Alaina, it struck him like a jolt. His memory was not proven false. Time had not diminished the young woman's beauty. His reaction was unlike what might be expected from the methodical, logical captain. Now he was simply a man returning to his lover. He was filled with the joy of her presence, the relief of her safety, and the sensuality of her being. However, the emotional tizzy, seething beneath the surface, was enough to cause the fringes of his vision to grow hazy. And as her high heeled shoes struck the stone footpath, they made a distinctive click that he focused on. A sense of excitement flooded over him, creating the desire to immediately seize hold of her. Despite his wish to run, he strode calmly along the intersecting causeway.

When she noticed him, she came to an abrupt stop. As she turned to face him, her surprise couldn't have been more pronounced. He could only guess that her emotional state was as elevated as his own.

Passersby might assume that they were acquaintances meeting casually to exchange friendly greetings. But his heart was pounding, and his palms were damp. A gust of wind blew a tangled lock of hair across his forehead, and he swiped it away absentmindedly.

"Henry!"

Her exclamation was short and sharp, giving him a start. As invariably happened, he fell under her mesmerizing spell, stammering, "I . . ., I . . ., I said, 'I'd be back.'"

Bridging the remaining gap between them in a few bounding steps, he reached out to put his arms around her, but she put her arms up and held him back.

"I thought you were dead!" she exclaimed, her face reflecting an emotional cocktail of flustered confusion and dismay.

Gallant stood transfixed. He had hoped her first reaction would be to throw her arms around him but would have understood a furious rant about how he had left her in limbo. He wasn't at all prepared for the icy stare she gave him.

Her voice was just as cold. "I've had no word from you for nearly a year."

"That wasn't my choice."

He searched for some soothing words. "I've thought of you every day we've been apart."

They stood frozen as seconds ticked by in slow motion—his eyes pleading, but her face an unreadable mask.

Losing his parents as a child had left Gallant a loner most of his life. His last relative, his grandmother, died during his first year at the academy—making him pretty much a loner and leaving him mystified by relationships.

Why is love so bewildering?

Aloud, he asked hesitantly, "Maybe you're not ready to forgive me, but can we at least be friends while you consider it?"

A million nanoseconds flittered by, and then, finally, she relented and smiled—a genuine smile.

That grin warmed him from the inside out. He felt a little weak in the knees and drew a deep breath to steady himself.

"You haven't changed," she said, biting her lower lip. "Why didn't you at least send word you were on the *Warrior*?"

"I wanted to see your face when you found out."

"Henry, I have to take this slow. I don't know exactly how I feel about you anymore."

Slow? Anymore?

"What do you mean?" He blushed and touched his cheek as if her verbal slap had been physical.

"I mean, we need to get reacquainted."

He heard the words she didn't say: she needed time before they could rediscover the passion they had once shared.

How much time?

Her expression struck him as unfamiliar, and Gallant wondered whether she sensed his inner turmoil and its cause. He felt vulnerable, exposed until he realized that he was projecting his own anxiety.

He gathered his composure. "What exactly do you mean?"

"Stop being pigheaded, Henry."

A smile twitched at the corner of his mouth. "Actually, you once said that 'pigheaded' was one of my more endearing qualities."

She put a hand over her mouth to suppress a chuckle, but immediately regretted her lapse. The frown returned.

He could see the storm clouds in her eyes. Levity was not the answer—he needed a new tactic. He said earnestly, "All right, Alaina. Slow it is. I'll behave, I promise. Let's get together tomorrow. Spend a little time to get reacquainted, as you suggest. Perhaps we could go for a hike in the jungle? Like we used to."

But she picked up on the implied intimacy.

"No," she shook her head. "Come to my house for dinner this weekend."

"Great," he said. But already his mind was imagining a boat trip to a neighboring island and a picnic on the beach.

She looked him up and down, considering, then turned to leave. "I'm on my way to the town hall to greet the captain of the *Warrior* and thank him for his help against the Titans."

"Then you're in luck. You've already found him."

"You?"

"Yes. Shall we walk together?"

Her face darkened. "The political balance here has shifted a great deal since you were last here."

From her posture and pained expression, he sensed a deep-seated problem. "In what way?" he asked, glad to step off the emotional rollercoaster.

"Just before you left, we threw out the ruling political party. But since then, a group surrounding Cyrus Wolf Jr. has coalesced into a solid block. It means trouble going forward."

CHAPTER 11

Achilles

"Sir, ships approaching Elysium," reported Midshipman Stedman, after bursting into the captain's cabin.

"Ships? What ships?"

"The cruiser *Achilles* and four destroyers are escorting a convoy of supply and transport ships, sir."

"Mr. Stedman, don't you think you should have been included those details in your initial statement? If I hadn't been monitoring the status screen, I could have assumed that you were reporting enemy ships were about to attack us. I might've hit the alarm."

"Ah . . . oh . . . yes, sir. Pardon, sir, I didn't think . . ."

"Exactly. What is their ETA?"

"Ah . . ."

"I'm certain the Officer of the Deck told you before he sent you. Didn't he?"

"Yes, sir. The estimated time of arrival is three

hours."

"Very well, Mr. Stedman. In the future, think about what your assignment entails before you proceed," said Gallant. He didn't want to badger the young man, just maximize his learning experiences.

"Aye aye, sir." The midshipman saluted sharply and left.

Gallant headed for the bridge behind him.

The *Achilles* was in the van of a column of destroyers. The ships had the latest FTL drive but lacked the stealth technology of the *Warrior*. When the convoy reached the planet, the auxiliary ships entered a low synchronous orbit. The warships took station high above them.

Since he had met with the Elysium Council, Gallant had been relentlessly working on repairs to his ship. Each day's overcrowded schedule required his personal attention. Despite his exhaustion, when the summons arrived, he knew his duty. He had to report to the captain of the *Achilles*, Commander Anton Neumann. The *Achilles* task force was behind schedule, and the captain was not likely to be in a cheerful mood.

When Gallant reflected on his career, Neumann was always there. His mind wandered over the perplexity of his strange relationship with this man—a rival in so many ways.

Our meetings are never pleasant.

Commander Anton Neumann was the quintessential genetically engineered officer. He was a direct contrast to Gallant's Natural talents. Even as a midshipman, Neumann had been petty, vindictive, and mean-spirited. But in battle, he had shown himself to be resolute, brave, and audacious. These wildly disparate traits were unsettling at best, at worst dangerously volatile.

Neumann's motives were more transparent now. He was terrified of his father. And gaining that man's approval was his sole purpose in life. The family's influential mining and shipping dynasty dominated the Solar System. He would stop at nothing to keep the family's empire intact. Gallant surmised they had ambitions for Elysium as well.

More perplexing was Neumann's marriage to Kelsey Mitchel. Why Kelsey had found him attractive was no mystery. He was handsome, rich, and accomplished in every aspect of social grace. And although Kelsey was beautiful and talented in her own right, why Neumann had picked her, out of all the women, he could have had, remained a mystery. Did Anton hope the respected name of Mitchel might lead to political advantages? Perhaps it was spite against Gallant, who had also pursued Kelsey. Could even Neumann be so petty as to destroy a young woman's dreams, just to ... to what?

The transport ships carried twenty thousand colonists, all employees of the NNR Corporation. They were tasked with establishing NNR's interests in the Tau Ceti system. Gallant noted another issue. The new arrivals were genetically engineered, while the Elysium colonists were Natural born.

The shuttle Gallant flew to the *Achilles* was a

less responsive craft than a fighter, but he enjoyed the short trip. The shuttle quivered as its tractor beam reached out to the cruiser, slowly drawing alongside. Once the docking hatch opened to admit him, a soldier escorted him to the bridge. He took the opportunity to look around the meticulous ship with marine guards at strategic posts. The glossy varnish of the bulkheads reflected more spit and polish than he had ever seen.

"Welcome aboard, Mr. Gallant. I'm the OOD," said a young woman in a spotless uniform.

"Thank you."

She continued, "Mr. Gallant, I know you. Do you remember me, sir?"

"Yes, I do. You were a plebe when I left the academy."

The OOD nodded, pleased. She turned to a junior midshipman and ordered, "Midshipman, take the commander to the captain's cabin."

They proceeded along a well-lit corridor, and after a few twists and turns, arrived at the captain's stateroom. It was a lavish affair compared to the tiny cabin Gallant occupied in the *Warrior*. The room featured extravagant trappings far beyond the means of a typical military officer.

He waited inside the open hatch. Neumann remained seated with his back to him, reviewing something on a computer screen. Clean-shaven with close-cropped hair, Neumann rapidly slid his finger across the screen. He seemed uninterested in his visitor.

Gallant squirmed inwardly at the affront.

Under Neumann's authority, no mistake was too small to be overlooked, no success too insignificant to be appropriated.

Will we ever find a way forward without antagonism?

Finally, Neumann dropped his air of impenetrable reserve and turned his attention to his visitor. "I've read your preliminary battle report with the Titan destroyer. What is your assessment of the current military situation?"

"Though I doubt they have any other ships in the system right now, I suspect they already have bases and satellites on the outer planets. I haven't enough information to assess their strength, but we would do well to eliminate them. Fleet command would naturally want to gather more intelligence from them."

Neumann asked, "Did you complete your mission in the Gliese-581 system?"

"Yes, sir. I've submitted my mission report to your XO, including an assessment of the Titans' possible FTL drive."

Then Gallant summarized the *Warrior's* status. He mentioned the damaged sub-light engine reactor core, stealth technology support systems failures, several cracks in the ship's hull, needed personnel replacements, and a required weapon system overhaul. He expressed his hope that Elysium's facilities would be made available to the ship.

An awkward silence followed. Once again, as so often over the past years, Gallant wondered why they could never find common ground.

After a few minutes, he asked, "How are you and Kelsey finding married life?"

Neumann flinched as if Gallant had struck him. His brilliant blue eyes hardened to ice. All the light left his face.

What happened?

Without looking up, Neumann said, "Dismissed."

CHAPTER 12

Date

After a fitful sleep filled with disturbing visions of violence and dark figures, Gallant woke in an ill temper. He spent several minutes in bed, stretching his aching muscles, before gathering himself to face the day. He rubbed his temples, then pushed himself upright and swung his feet to the ground.

A cold shower somewhat revived him, and he extended his normal military allotment of water by several minutes. Slowly, his scowl softened to a more neutral acceptance of the day. Dressing, he suddenly smiled and picked up his pace when he remembered he was going to see Alaina. He regretted the chill that had come between them and that she was not as open to him as before. He longed for her laughter and the instant understanding they had once enjoyed.

He took a shuttle to the planet.

Bounding along the narrow cobblestone

streets with their overhanging shade trees and quaint colonial cottages, he breathed deeply of Elysium's fresh air. It was a pleasant change from his shipboard's metallic life.

His good humor swelled as he approached Alaina's home, a simple colonial two-story house on the road with similar wooden cottages. A broad veranda overlooked the surrounding garden and well-pruned shrubbery. Hurrying up the steps, Gallant saw several women passersby in summer dresses and men in gray work clothes. They waved a pleasant greeting to him.

Despite its rustic appearance, the house boasted sophisticated in-home AI technology. Before he even knocked, the door scanned him, recognized him, and automatically opened, announcing his arrival.

Alaina appeared before he had taken two steps into the living room. The red blouse and a pale green skirt suited his mood; she looked bright and vivid, like the Alaina he remembered.

He grinned, "I've been looking forward to today. I hope I'm welcome?"

"Of course, you're welcome," she leaned forward and gave him a peck on the cheek. "I'm even ready to forgive you for your unforgivable absence."

"I've missed you," she said with a smile.

He brightened. The words filled him up. "I could ask for no more."

"Did you miss me?"

"Every minute," he said, laying his hand lightly

on her arm.

"You're happy now?"

"Yes, I can't feel unhappy when we're together."

For a long moment, she was silent. Then with another glance up at him, she said, "I've decided that delaying seeing you was punishing me as much as you."

"So, dinner is your solution?"

"Yes."

"I'm glad. I'm very glad."

She turned toward a mirror and adjusted her hair, watching as his reflection approached. For a second, their eyes met in the mirror. A smile spread from her eyes to her lips. She turned and said with unrestrained gaiety, "Control yourself. It distresses me when you become muddled with excitement."

She likes me again!

He said, "For that, I'm glad."

They engaged in light banter for several minutes and then adjourned to the dining room, where she laid out their small feast.

The table was set with her best plates and accessories, with honeycomb and fragrant flowers adding to the pleasing effect. Through the open windows, he heard the island sounds—wind rustling through the trees, the chirping of nesting birds, and the strident cries of small creatures scurrying about for a meal.

Alaina described the preparation of each dish, proud of her accomplishment. Gallant made ingratiating sounds, which she acknowledged appreciatively.

He lost count of the courses and knew he would have to double his physical fitness regimen for the next week to make up for the indulgence. But it was the best meal he'd ever eaten—the good food exceeded only by the charming company.

They took their time eating, enjoying animated conversation interspersed with comfortable silences. Although both had much to say, each was wary of broaching sensitive subjects.

Elbows on the table, resting her chin on her clasped hands, Alaina recounted the events of the past year on Elysium. Eventually, she prodded Gallant into talking about his ship and crew, though he insisted he didn't want to bore her with details about life in space.

They spoke of day-to-day activities, and although the subjects weren't important, he felt encouraged. They exchanged personal confidences that reestablished some of their past bond and connection.

"Are you still painting?" Gallant asked after another lull.

"Yes. It is my exquisite pleasure. Would you like to see my latest work?"

"Of course."

She led him to her studio. Several new paintings showed the countryside, with figures of the children and people of Halo. He examined them and commented on her improved style. A series of nude statues sculpted he knew by Liam, caught his eye, and he noted with satisfaction that there were no new ones in the collection.

"What is Earth-like now?"

"I didn't spend any time on Earth. I did visit Mars while the *Warrior* was being outfitted. It's not the same as when I was growing up. There's a lot of war pain due."

"Do you still communicate with Kelsey, your long-lost love?"

He was surprised that she asked about his former romance but hesitated only a moment.

"She's married. I told you she was engaged. She married Anton Neumann some months ago."

"What happened between you?"

He frowned despite himself, and she noticed.

He said slowly, "I don't know. We didn't seem to want the same things."

"Oh. And are you on better terms with Commander Neumann now?"

Gallant looked uncomfortable. "Well . . . I don't know. We may never be on better terms."

"Let's go out on the veranda."

They walked out into the warm evening. Her mood seemed to lift, and she hummed a tune.

She felt him watching her, and her cheeks heated up.

There's a freshness about her. She almost seems brand new.

"Do you know that we've been separated longer than we've been together?" she asked.

He nodded and sighed.

She turned abruptly and looked at him. "Would you like to come with me to the celebration on Thursday?"

"Well, yes. I'd love to go with you, though you will know everyone, and I will be the stranger," he said.

"The new colonists and crews from the ships will be there, too, so I won't know everyone either."

"What time should I come by and pick you up? We could go together?"

Her eyes darkened, and he thought she might rebuke him. Instead, she remained quiet for a long moment.

His brow furrowed in dismay.

"Henry, I must be perfectly honest with you. I was serious when I said we need to take our relationship slow," she said.

A chill swept over him as his imagination spun to unpleasant possibilities. He longed to see their future intact, hated to leave with their relationship still so uncertain. But her expression remained stony.

She said, "Be here at seven."

He said, "I should go."

"Till Tuesday at seven, then."

"Till then."

CHAPTER 13

Mining Venture

Rain shimmered through the warm Halo air. The showers had been constant since dawn, but in the town hall, six men gathered around a table in the conference room, oblivious to the dreary weather. They had already wined and dined, a sumptuous meal consisting of a cream soup dish, some mutton, a meat, and sweetbreads pie. That was followed by raw fish with assorted greens, as well as cheese and nuts. A glass of sherry had satiated even the most demanding palate.

Councilman Reverend Thibodaux set down his coffee. Next to him sat Gregory Rothschild, the NNR corporate financial manager and banker whose sour face matched his tedious profession. The leader of the manufacturing syndicate was next—a rather sparse man with gray hair and a well-trimmed beard. Finally, William Treadwell, senior mining engineer and leader of the miner's consortium took his seat. In contrast to the others, he had an eager-to-please face. He was surprisingly jolly disposition with pudgy cheeks and twinkling eyes. These men represented the key associations that would decide how to allocate the planet's scant manpower and machinery resources.

Gallant and Chief Howard joined the group to discuss reopening the mining operations at the foot of the Brobdingnag Volcano. The rich mineral deposits were dispersed over several mountain ranges. They included essential minerals needed to manufacture steel and semiconductors, as well as fissionable metals for nuclear reactions. That was everything needed to both refit the *Warrior* and build defenses for the planet.

"Mr. Gallant, I'm pleased you've come. Good to have you back," said Treadwell.

"Thank you. I'm glad to be here." He jumped right into the fray. "We're here to discuss preliminary allotment of work and funding to upgrade the Elysium mining and manufacturing facilities, which will benefit the people of Elysium and hopefully provided the much-needed repair and replacement parts for the *Warrior*."

"Well," said Treadwell, "I, for one, regret that we closed down the mining operations several months ago. It was a rather hasty decision based on cost and manpower limitations. Now it's clear that planetary security trumps narrow financial interests." He smiled and added, "I'm looking forward to working closely with Chief Howard and his engineering team on how best to staff and operate the mining works."

Howard replied, "I'm glad to hear that you're willing to direct the operations to our mutual needs. There's much to do. The *Achilles* task force has helped by providing spare parts and extra manpower. The *Warrior's* repair schedule will still take two or more months of hard work."

Rothschild gave a dry cough. "Naturally, the NNR Corporation has its own needs, but we are willing to defer to Chief Howard's priorities and Treadwell's mining expertise."

Treadwell said, "Mining operations require drilling, blasting, and transporting a variety of materials. That doesn't even address the need to crush, grind, and process them for production. Because of our limited time and manpower, we'll need to incorporate as much remote automation as possible. Sensors can provide data for remote control operations. That will reduce human labor. However, these devices do require a large capital investment."

He stopped for a moment and spat a vile brown substance into a cup. He was clearly unaccustomed to making long statements. He would have preferred to just get on with the job instead of sitting around talking about it.

He continued, "The robotic mining equipment will dig shafts using smart drills. It can sense what type of materials they're drilling through. Another advantage of this technology is safety. We'll be able to limit the miners' exposure to dangerous conditions, like unstable terrain, blast areas, and falling debris. In the end, automation will be the least expensive option. On the other hand, we don't have enough expert equipment operators. So, we'll have to train more, and that takes time."

Again, he paused and looked as though he would spit again, but stopped and concluded, "Sorry, but that's how it is."

"Well," said Chief Howard, "I, for one, am willing to follow Treadwell's recommendation. Sounds like he knows what he's talking about."

Treadwell glowed from the praise. He winked at Howard and chuckled, "Naturally, I'll defer to the top engineering mind from the *Warrior.* He knows everything about calibrating and maintaining the automated equipment."

The rest of the men murmured an amicable agreement.

Treadwell said, "I also have some good news to share from the mine. We've uncovered a new vein of rich ore. I believe the profit margin will expand to everyone's satisfaction."

There were more smiles around the table.

He added, "However, it looks like we'll have a lot of water near the new vein, which, as you know, means the additional headache of pumping it out. And we have one other significant problem—a recent collapse in the secondary shaft of the main mine."

Nonetheless, they toasted the discovery with a glass of fermented juice the locals had made. It was somewhat more potent than the brewery stock they normally relied on.

"I can supply some excavation machinery to remove the debris," Rothschild offered.

"Very admirable of you, I'm sure," said Reverend Thibodaux.

The talk shifted to technical production needs. Howard outlined what ores and tonnage would be required to produce the *Warrior's* needed parts. Next came a discussion on the production of missiles and satellites for Elysium's protection that had already been postponed.

Gallant cleared his throat and said, "Here's our production plan and schedule in detail." He had designed his plan to foster maximum cooperation between the parties. Even so, they would still be well short of the equipment they ultimately needed—this was only the initial outlay.

There was a moment of silence. Now he would find out whether he had succeeded. He searched their faces.

Treadwell said, "I'm willing to work as an engineering supervisor without pay until we get the business back into operation."

Rothschild said, "I can cover startup costs to help finance the machinery upgrades and worker salaries. As for the heavy machinery, we'll need help from the United Planets task force. NNR's supplies are currently being off-loaded."

Gallant said, "That sounds workable. I'm confident that we can begin making repairs immediately with what we have. Although I'm sure we'll run into problems as we progress, we can expect the *Achilles* task force to help."

Treadwell unfastened his collar button and wiped the sweat off his forehead. He said, "I agree. That's reasonable."

Rothschild interrupted, "I'm worried about the initial costs being recovered at an adequate profit. You know that without profit, we'll lose investors."

Gallant waved his hand dismissively as if none of that mattered. "Using autonomous mining vehicles will reduce the footprint of the operation while improving productivity and vehicle utilization. That will help keep costs down, I'm sure."

Treadwell added, "I've already inspected the mines and production factories. They're laid out with good roads between them so that automated vehicles can move material back and forth."

Howard asked, "How deep does the main mine shaft go?"

The mining engineer scratched his head and thought for a moment. He said, "It reaches four kilometers into the ground and extends several kilometers to the west under the jungle. The pumps work overtime to remove the water that seeps in. If we could pump faster, then we could go after the rich vein that goes off toward the ocean." He pointed to the map. "See, here's a streak of material worth mining, but air compressors are needed at this level."

Rothschild said, "You've seen our cost estimates. We couldn't make a new vein cost-effective at that grade of ore."

"The NNR Corporation will supply us with

some needed equipment and small gear," said Rothschild. "I will arrange the financing and shepherd the necessary passage through the legal proceedings."

"We will divide the shares among the interested parties," said Gallant, looking around the table triumphantly.

Rothschild said, "We've worked out the costs and manpower requirements so as not to overtax the fragile Halo economy. Thanks to the generosity of the NNR Corporation, credit and major equipment procurement won't be a problem. NNR will, of course, expect an appropriate share of the venture to offset its risks."

Gallant listened as the businessmen explored the remaining issues: credit, expenditures, debts, and potential insolvency and liquidation, all issues a sailor knew little about.

Rothschild summed up, "We need to open up investment opportunities to the NNR colonists, too. I'm sure they will want to be involved and share the risks as well as the rewards. Creating credits and financing through a UP banking conglomerate supported by NNR will allow that option. NNR is prepared to offer us everything we need for this endeavor."

He paused, as if gauging the mood of the room, and added, "The share NNR has in mind is a mere forty percent stake in the enterprise. NNR will also purchase land near Halo to build a new settlement. From there, they can supplement labor as needed. In addition, they wish to purchase land in the volcano rich region to develop their own mining operations."

He looked at the faces around the table and concluded, "I think NNR is most generous."

Gallant suspected that NNR expected to dominate all the mining and manufacturing operations on New Kauai. He said, "I suggest that, if in the future, any of our investors are interested in selling their stakes, NNR offers us the right of first refusal at their price."

"Good idea."

With that, Gallant asked, "What do you say, gentlemen? Do we have a deal?"

As a show of good faith, Gallant bought into the company with every penny he had in his meager savings account. He never had much of an opportunity to spend his slight salary over his six years of service. It was enough to take a one-tenth of one-percent share in the venture. The other businessmen distributed the rest between them, with NNR holding the largest share of forty percent.

"At last, we are all agreed. Let's raise our glasses in a toast of fellowship to our great endeavor," said Treadwell, his voice cheery.

"Despite past adversities, we may yet reap prosperity," said Reverend Thibodaux. "Gentlemen, shall we vote to accept the proposal? Those in favor signify by saying, 'aye.'"

"Aye."

"Aye."

"Aye."

"Aye."

Gallant and Howard added the final "ayes" to

carry the vote forward.

Treadwell said, "The work will begin just as soon as the men are gathered, and the orders are given."

Gallant was satisfied that he could work well with the civilian authorities and cooperate with them to repair his ship.

He said, "We've sat as equals in this discussion, and I appreciate that we will bear equal responsibility in the success or failure of the endeavor."

Treadwell said, "I propose a toast."

They all raised their glasses.

"To the Brobdingnag mine!"

"To Elysium!"

"To the *Warrior!*"

They drained their glasses.

Less than twenty-four hours later, Gregory Rothschild made offers, on behalf of the NNR Corporation, to acquire a greater percentage of the mining operation by pressuring several of the participants.

CHAPTER 14

Celebration

A s with most of the important events in Halo, the town's people gathered in the forty-acre common area of Freedom Park, landscaped with small trees and rustic boulders, located at the junction of the town's three main roads. One road ran the length of the island from east to west. A second ran north toward the mountainous volcanoes. The remaining road forked to the southeast toward the ocean shore with its high cliffs and many caves. At the edge of the park, there was a picturesque lighthouse facing the ocean at an acute angle. The focal point for the colonists' historic proceedings, the park was just a short walk from the town hall.

The crowd arrived in vehicles that lined the roads and were parked haphazardly. Many inhabitants preferred to walk the short distance from their houses along the radial walkways, which stuck out like spokes in a wheel. Banners decorated the arbors inside the park, proclaiming a celebration for the victory over the Titans and the near doubling of the planet's population. The Elysium Council had already issued permits for the NNR Corporation to build homes for the new arrivals on the western half of the island.

On their way to the park, Gallant and Alaina gazed around the town with its quaint little houses and tree-lined lanes. The narrow winding streets were crowded. When Alaina saw people she knew, she stopped to greet them. They passed by several out-of-the-way cottages and noticed an old woman standing in the doorway of one. She waved pleasantly.

Gallant and Alaina waved back.

When they reached the park, they joined the feast that had been prepared to celebrate the military victory. But the atmosphere was deceptively pleasant.

The original colonists occupied the eastern half of the island and lived mainly within Halo. And on the surface, the native population welcomed the arrival of protective warships and the influx of new settlers. But there was an undercurrent of concern about the disorienting changes these events forecast.

CHAPTER 15

A Prudent Man

The sun had set, and a salty breeze blew in from the ocean. Four mineworkers drove a tractor up a steep mountain road toward the Brobdingnag mine. They passed through the manufacturing site where the factory chimneys spewed dirty yellow and black soot into the pristine Elysium air. Workers bent to their tasks around the site. Most of them wore the bright green-and-black coveralls of NNR men, with just a few local townspeople mixed in.

The tractor trundled by a storage area brimming with ore for processing, but at the last minute, they stopped in front of a man slouched on a wooden crate in the shade of a gnarled tree. He was of average height and older than most of the workers, but strongly built. His gray coveralls, dirty shirt, and heavy industrial boots were worn and scuffed. His jacket pockets bulged with odds and ends, including a few stray tools. He sat idly, whittling and whistling merrily to himself.

The leader of the tractor, a tall thin man with beady eyes, shut off his machine, and the others followed suit. In the deafening quiet that followed, he said, "Good day. Are you the yard foreman?"

The older man scratched his nose. "Maybe."

Raising his hands as a gesture of impatience, the leader asked, "Come on. Are you, or aren't you?"

"Well, now, I'm really not sure. You NNR types have taken to doing things your own way, never mind what I say."

"Look, we're not looking for trouble. We just need directions to the new excavation site. We've been assigned to work there."

The older man glanced suspiciously at them, but after a minute, he jerked a thumb up the hill toward the peak of the mighty volcano. "There. That path will take you to the new dig site."

The tractor crew headed out without another word.

The old man grumbled a little and spat into the dirt but didn't get up from his wooden crate. Several birds pecked at a branch over his head. The noise of heavy machinery rumbled in the distance. He resumed his whittling and whistling.

Soon Gallant arrived on the site and approached the old man. He said, "Hello, Treadwell. It's good to see you again."

The mining engineer nodded but kept whittling and said nothing.

"Do we have any engineering problems? Cave-ins? Equipment malfunctions?"

"No, we're able to handle those glitches just fine whenever they pop up."

"Trouble with mineral exploration?"

"Nope. The new vein is providing excellent yield."

"What about fabrication or manufacturing problems?"

"Well, those are outside my responsibility, but as far as I can tell, they're going well enough."

Exasperated, Gallant snapped, "Then why did you send word saying you wanted to see me?"

"You're the captain. Everyone wants to see you."

Beginning to lose patience, he fixed a piercing look on the engineer. "Treadwell?"

The older man sighed and finally stopped whittling. His face contorted, but the sneer couldn't hide his fierce pride. He snorted one word, "People."

Aware of the man's stoic nature, Gallant asked, "I know that you always say what you think, so tell me: Are the NNR personnel cooperating with the local workmen?"

"Hah!" he barked. "That's not served me so well, saying what comes to mind. Sometimes people aren't happy to hear it."

"I hope you know me well enough to speak frankly."

"Still, a prudent man marks his words."

Gallant waited.

Treadwell sighed, "You're young—still full of piss and vinegar. The trouble is, very few men can stay tough by the time they're old. They've been knocked down by life's troubles. Old age tends to soften you up."

"Don't kid me, William, you're as tough an old bird as ever was."

The man's wrinkled face smiled up, and he looked Gallant up and down. "None."

"Pardon?"

"There's no cooperation—like I said—none."

Hoping for some insight, Gallant asked, "Do you have time to give me a tour?"

"That'd be fine."

Treadwell took him around the camp. Everything appeared to be well-run. The ore was being extracted and hauled to the appropriate stockpiles. The smelting plant was producing metal at a record pace, and the fabrication plant was turning out product smoothly. The entire operation appeared to be running efficiently.

But Gallant noticed some inconsistencies. All the new automated mining equipment was being operated the NNR control center, not Treadwell's supervisor shack. The drivers of the specialized vehicles were also all NNR men, smiling pleasantly. The native workers all seemed to be in drudgery jobs, mostly hard labor. He didn't see happy faces there.

Gallant asked, "I thought the plan was to train the natives to work in the high-tech jobs?"

Treadwell chewed on his lip but said nothing.

As they headed back to Gallant's vehicle, a young man wearing clean green-and-black coveralls approached them.

"Hello, Mr. Gallant, I'm the foreman here. Can I help you?"

"No, thank you, Mr. Treadwell has taken good care of me."

The young man smiled at Gallant, nodded at Treadwell, and left without saying anything else.

Treadwell spat on the ground and said, "Like I said—none."

CHAPTER 16

Sailing

Aquamarine waves frothed on the shore while puffy white clouds drifted through the azure sky. On the horizon, the last wisps of morning fog faded from view behind a light breeze. Gallant walked into the marina and saw Alaina standing at the end of a pier, her gaze fixed on the sea. She wore a white halter and tan shorts. Her hair was pulled back in a ponytail, tied with a yellow ribbon. He stood for a minute, content to simply watch her.

A warm gust of wind woke him from his reverie. He walked along the wharf, stopping several meters behind her.

"Alaina?"

Startled, she jumped and turned her head. Her eyes brightened with delight.

"Henry!"

"I'm sorry. I shouldn't have come up behind you like that."

"No, not at all. It was silly of me—my mind was far away."

"You look wonderful."

"Thank you."

An incoming wave shattered against the nearby rocks, spraying them with seawater.

"You wouldn't go hiking in the jungle with me, but decided sailing was a lesser evil?"

"Yes," she laughed—an infectious, happy laugh.

The marina was crowded with both fishing and pleasure boats. Alaina's fifteen-meter yawl, the *Haven*, was at the end of the pier. They climbed aboard and began unfurling the jib sail. Gallant hauled in the bowline while Alaina cast off the stern line. The jib billowed and caught the wind, and they headed out.

He removed a line from its cleat to raise the mainsail while yanking at the furling line of the jib. He secured the boom in its cradle and sat down in the cockpit. As he heaved on the helm to point the bow toward open water, they had to traverse a seaweed patch. When they had gone a hundred meters, he pulled the sheets taut and let the boat heel over.

They skirted a sandbar and passed the cliffs where a lighthouse stood watch high above the bay. Waves battered the jagged rocks that ringed the shore, sending up spray that shimmered in the morning light.

He had the feeling the trip was a fresh start, a new adventure, and wondered whether she felt the same. But he said nothing, afraid to ask anything that might disturb the delicate balance between them. He leaned against the tiller to turn the boat toward the open sea, away from New Kauai.

The *Haven* clawed her way down the bay toward a string of small, deserted islands to the east, picking up speed ahead of the seaward breeze. A westerly wind laid her over as she responded to Gallant's hand at the helm. The blustery summer wind sang in his ears as the boat pitched forward and then rolled as a wave broke against her hull. The *Haven* and the sea synchronized into a thrashing rhythm—pitch—roll—pitch—roll, while in the distance, several other small craft ran before the wind. He savored the majesty of the vivid sunlight and writhing seas, but even so, today, he was distracted by Alaina's delicate silhouette as she stood at the mast, grasping the rigging while her streaming blonde hair acted as a telltale.

"Alaina," he yelled over the gusty weather—beckoning her aft. She smiled, and balancing herself against the undulation of the deck, made her way to the cockpit. She sat sideways to him—her knees tucked under her, a gay expression on her face.

He sailed the boat closer to the wind to gain speed, and the wind greeted him with new enthusiasm. The splash and swish of the water against the hull made a chorus of sea noises that attracted the local inhabitants. A school of fish kept pace with the boat, leaping and twisting through the waves as if the yawl was one of them.

Seeing that Alaina's zeal for adventure hadn't waned, he reached toward her, and pulled her close.

"You love it, don't you?" she asked, snuggling against him. "Sailing, I mean."

"It's grand—sometimes tranquil, sometimes harsh, but always exhilarating."

"I didn't know that you had so many chances to sail on Mars."

"Ha," he laughed. "Terraformed Mars offers nearly all the amenities of Earth, though on a modest scale."

They sailed for an hour until they approached a tiny, deserted island with white beaches and a secluded cove.

He loosened the sails and turned, letting the waves carry the *Haven* toward the shore. He dropped the anchor as the boat slipped through the rippling water and gently scraped on the sandy bottom. Quickly furling the sails, he jumped over the side and turned to lift Alaina off. He carried her through the rolling surf, thrilling to the feel of her arms around his neck. She didn't protest at all when he kissed her. Her lips pressed back with equal intent.

Gallant breathed in her musky scent, reminding him of their past adventures. Wordlessly, he returned to the boat for their goods.

He spread a blanket out on the sand while Alaina opened the picnic basket. She laid out a tempting lunch, but they ate little, too engrossed in each other to be hungry.

Before today, she had seemed to be two people —one his lover, the other a stranger. His eyes searched her face, and what he saw gave him hope. He could separate the two, or better yet wear away the distinction until only his lover was left.

He asked, "How about a swim?"

"I didn't bring a bathing suit."

"That was never a problem before."

As a smile spread across her lips, he knew it wasn't a problem now.

"You're a bad boy," she said, giving his arm a slap.

"I can be." He wondered if she knew that she was the cause of that.

They stripped and jumped into the surf, swimming out from the shore a good distance. Turning parallel to the beach, they doubled back. They flopped down on their blanket, exhilarated and exhausted.

They watched as the incoming tide washed away their footprints. A flurry of spray splattered over them.

Alaina lay back on the blanket, comfortable with her nudity. When he dropped beside her, she rolled over—her lips moist and parted—and kissed him. He wrapped his arms around her, electrified at her immediate response. Their passion rose and blossomed as their lovemaking filled the afternoon. Afterward, they lay together, not moving, content in each other's presence for a long time.

Gazing at the sunbaked sand and the glimmering blue water, Gallant dismissed the past from his mind. Instead, he focused on the immediate future. He was certain of only one thing—he never wanted to lose this woman. He knew they belonged together, now, and always.

"Are you cold?" he asked.

"No." She snuggled comfortably into his arms.

"I love you, Henry," she whispered. The words anchored him to her world.

"I love you, Alaina."

"Because?"

"Because it's too hard not to."

The sex had always been good between them. Only the separation kept getting in their way.

They fell asleep. An hour later, Gallant woke up with Alaina still asleep beside him. He touched her and she woke, smiling, and reached for him.

Her touch sent a jolt through him, and she laughed at the look on his face. She rolled away from him coyly, so he put his arm over her and nuzzled the back of her neck, feeling the shiver run through her as his lips explored her salty skin. After a moment, she twisted around to face him, eager to resume their lovemaking. Again, their passion echoed the crashing of the waves on the shore. In the breathless aftermath, they lay quietly entwined, watching the ocean swells caress the horizon.

"I have a keepsake for you." She sat up to rummage through the picnic basket and handed him a small locket pin with a picture of herself inside.

He cradled the locket in his palm, searching for words to convey his emotion. "I'll keep your charm near me and treasure it always."

"Is your life charmed?"

"It must be, or I'd be long dead. Though possibly, I am already, and this is heaven."

Before long, he sat up to scan the sky and asked, "Home now?"

"Just a little longer. The afternoon is so grand. I want to make it last as long as possible."

Bleary-eyed, he blinked the sand from his eyes and peered at the sea.

"The wind's picking up," he said. He hesitated, cherishing each moment of the day. "I think we'd better head back."

Alaina nodded, and slowly they dressed and packed up their gear. Together they got the yawl out of the surf and made their way back to sea.

The *Haven* layover before the strengthening wind, waves crashing and hissing over the railing. A wild gust of air almost took her aback, and she bucked until Gallant pushed down the helm to let her pay off. Then she steadied and thrashed through the swells toward the harbor.

The sun was just setting when they docked in the New Kauai harbor.

CHAPTER 17

Repairs

T he *Warrior* was a special ship—the only stealth vessel in the United Planet's fleet—a marvel of the most advanced science. Its FTL drive and advanced weaponry had propelled it to the forefront of the war against the Titans. The crew's expertise was the outgrowth of multiple hazardous missions and battles. But now, the *Warrior* was anything but pretty. Her recent battle action left her and her crew sorely wanting.

An image of Neumann's face barking flashed through Gallant's mind—leaving him dumbfounded as he considered the deplorable state of repairs.

After cursing for what seemed an excessive period, he pressed the intercom and ordered, "Have Mr. Roberts and Chief Howard report to my stateroom, immediately."

He disregarded the startled reply, "Ah, . . .huh, aye aye, sir."

He became agitated while he waited. He scrolled through screens of equipment status read-outs, most of which had not been updated in several days.

Roberts was the first to arrive. He tugged at his incorrectly buttoned jacket and swiped at the grease stains on his shirt collar. He pulled a bulging gear part from his pants pocket and looked furtively for a place to drop it.

Surprised at the appearance of his normally meticulous XO, Gallant stared without speaking as he tried to sort out what he needed to ask.

Since the ship-to-ship battle, Roberts had been invaluable in getting the battered shell of the *Warrior* into a useful condition. He had been eager, alert, and diligent. Still, the ship remained rife with broken pipes, damaged equipment, and wrenched bulkheads. There was an unmistaken urgency in the air, as the sweat of every man aboard poured into each cubby hole throughout the ship. Their work was under grueling conditions. Now, the normally organized ship was cluttered and chaotic. Various equipment and machinery were either being taken apart or being tested.

Roberts squirmed under Gallant's silent unrelenting stare. His eyes dropped down to the floor as he tried to wipe some of the grime from his shoes. He said, "Please pardon my appearance, sir. I was engaged in a calibration test in the engine room."

"That doesn't matter right now. I'd like to . . .," Gallant stopped. He found himself caught with nothing more intelligent to add. He fell into thought and kept his eyes fixed on his XO, which prevented Roberts from recovering his equanimity.

Chief Howard appeared at the doorway and knocked. He was out of uniform—wearing instead, a heavy protective hazmat suit that was covered with odd chemicals and black soot. He, too, appeared self-conscious about making a mess in the captain's cabin.

Coming under Gallant's stare, Howard bowed his head and muttered, "You wanted to see me, sir?"

"Yes," Gallant said, but he didn't know how to continue. Finally, he said, "From what I see throughout the ship, things are woefully behind and disorganized."

Howard looked at Roberts, who looked back at him.

Roberts started, "That's so, sir. I, huh . . ."

Gallant cut in, "Why, are we unable to get the parts we need. Even the ship's stores, and supplies are out of date. And the testing schedule is completely fouled up. Neither of you has updated the status reports and I can't make any sense out the critical timeline schedule."

"Well, uh, . . ., I, uh, sir," began Roberts, stuttering.

"Why are you reporting deferring repairs that will delay deployment?"

"I uh . . ., you see, sir, the logistics of completing manufactured parts and transporting them to the ship. And the installing and tests has not always gone well. Some parts had to be rejected, and new molds cast. Some redesign was also necessary, . . .," fumbled Howard.

Roberts added, "Yes, sir, and we are short of specialized types of installation equipment that we would find in a major shipyard. We've improvised, but . . ."

"What? Are we short of workers for installation?" asked Gallant, standing up.

"I was going to speak to you about that . . ." said, Roberts, taking a step back.

"You mean with all the planet's resources, we are so fouled up, we can't meet our mission requirements?"

"Uh."

"Look at this computer readout," demanded Gallant, pointing to the screen.

The two subordinates blushed and stammered through several more minutes, as Gallant listed their shortcomings.

Finally, he asked, "What is the defensive posture of this ship? If we were attacked today, what do you expect would happened?"

"We are unable to maneuver, or raise shields, sir. We have no operational weapons systems at present. However, I hope to have the shields available before the end of the day," muttered Roberts.

"I'm shocked. Why have you allowed this ship to remain defenseless?" asked Gallant.

"No excuse, sir," said Roberts, hanging his head.

Gallant opened and closed his mouth one more time before he blushed and reconsidered his complaint. Mentally, he took himself to task for his failure to diligently follow progress on the *Warrior*. Sweat broke out on his neck, and he realized he had been remiss in tracking the ship's status. His mounting anger, he realized, was not actually with these men who had been working tirelessly while he was absent. It was his absence that left too much for others, when it was he, who was needed to make critical decisions and guide the process.

The crux of the matter was that his men had been working while he was away, and he felt guilty at the state of affairs. His head was spinning as he went over the arguments multiple times but always arrived at the same conclusion.

What's my excuse for lack of oversight of my own ship?

He condemned himself for his inattention. He tried to rationalize his time planet-side by the explicit need to establish the manufacturing facilities for the repair parts. But he couldn't blame all his inattention to profession duties elsewhere. He blushed when he thought of Alaina. She had been a strong temptation, but that was no excuse. He couldn't rationalize the distraction she had become.

He was still angry—only now—the anger was direct at himself.

He said to Roberts, "Have Officers Call in the wardroom in thirty minutes. We'll work together to get things better organized. I would appreciate it if you would attend, Chief."

Both men responded, "Aye aye, sir,"

The only way he could absolve his guilt and disappointment was to immerse himself in corrective action. A burst of herculean energy flowed through him, and he began addressing the difficulties. He plugged into the AI interface and immersed his mind in everything the data could provide. He began considering what action to take first and how to integrate time, material, and men into a coherent plan.

By the time the officers of the *Warrior* gathered around the wardroom table, Gallant was ready to redirect their work schedule.

"Be seated, gentlemen," said Gallant, his eyes passing over each face. "I regret to say that I am displeased with the current state of ship repairs, though I must confess to bearing much of the blame since urgent business kept me planet-side longer than anticipated."

He felt a twinge of guilt for the white lie of omitting his personal dalliance.

He said, "We have a big push coming. We're going to carry the war to the Titans. That's what this ship was specially built for. That's what we've been training and why we've got to get repairs and a shakedown cruise completed as soon as possible. I know each of you is as anxious to get going to accomplish this as I am, so here is my updated schedule and personnel assignments."

He displayed his report on the forward viewscreen. Line by line, he identified critical equipment repairs and those responsible for installation and testing. He showed a detailed critical timeline schedule.

"That's an ambitious workload, but I believe in you and this crew. We can do it. We will do it," he said, smacking his hand down on the table, "Do I have your support?"

There was a pregnant pause for a second, maybe two, then a rousing chorus of, "Yes, sir."

"Yes, sir."

"You can count on us, Skipper."

CHAPTER 18

Immigrants

I n Halo's Freedom Park, most of the island's citizens gathered for a town meeting.

Alaina raised her hands and asked to be heard over the roar of the crowd. She said, "Twenty-one years ago, the Titans kidnapped our people from an asteroid colony in the Solar System and transported them to this planet. We rebelled and drove them out, making this world our home. For the last two decades, we've been united in our struggle to create a society that reflects our values and dreams."

She looked around the gathering at the faces of people. Then she cast her gaze at councilmembers at the forefront. She said, "Now that new settlers have arrived, and we have welcomed them, it is our responsibility to assimilate them."

She paused and took a deep breath, knowing her next words would be controversial. "I propose that we lease them land for their homes and businesses and establish a path to citizenship for them."

There was a discontented murmur throughout the crowd.

She continued doggedly. "This plan will ensure a smooth and peaceful transition, integrating the new arrivals with minimal disruption to our way of life."

Wolfe stood up and thundered, "No!"

A crowd of observers, as well as many of the councilmembers, stood with him, echoing, "No! No!"

Alaina pleaded for order. As the shouting subsided, Wolfe added, "That approach is too slow. It's unacceptable to the new arrivals and to our society, which will benefit from their rapid integration."

Many around town meeting nodded in agreement, encouraging him to continue, "We should welcome the new arrivals as equals. They have the ships, supplies, and resources to turn this place into a paradise."

"It's already a paradise," Alaina argued. Many of the people agreed with her and were glad she spoke out for them.

Wolfe said, "I have an alternative proposal." He paused for dramatic effect. "We should grant them immediate citizenship and cede the western half of New Kauai to them."

Alaina's face paled. "Such action would effectively give control of our government to the NNR Corporation. It would diminish our own citizens' rights."

"I have the personal assurances of Commander Neumann, son of the president of NNR, that will not happen. He merely wants to facilitate the transition to ensure the industrial capacity is prepared for any further Titan threat."

"We don't have to take such precipitous action," said a member of the crowd.

"It's to everyone's benefit to act quickly. I call the council to vote on my suggestion," said Wolfe, a triumphant glint in his eye.

Alain said, "We should hold a referendum on this measure."

The crowd loudly supported the suggestion.

The council voted to set a date for the referendum.

Wolf frowned, but already his furrowed brows showed he was forming a plan.

CHAPTER 19

Lioness

It was strange for the two women to face each other across the wardroom table, eyes locked. McCall was challenging but curious, Alaina was wary but fearless.

With a fretful glance, Gallant left the women alone in the wardroom. He ushered several Elysium councilmembers on a tour of the *Warrior*.

McCall leaned back in her chair and said, "Henry has spoken of you often."

She dropped a spoonful of sugar into her coffee and stirred it slowly and methodically, clockwise, her eyes unwavering.

"That's odd," said Alaina, "he's never mentioned you."

She stared at the SIA agent, appraising her from every possible angle.

McCall's well-tailored uniform hugged her flawless figure, making her seem powerful. Alaina's simple short skirt and white blouse made her appear less so.

In truth, neither woman was comfortable.

"I can see why he finds you attractive," said McCall. "Though his weakness is his failure to nurture relationships. I think he would confess to that."

"You're wasting your breath telling me about Henry's faults. I know them all too well."

McCall chortled. She rose from her seat and walked closer. "You amuse me. What are you thinking? About events that never were? Or deeds that might be?"

Alaina shoved back from the table and stalked to the other side of the room, then turned to face the other woman defiantly. "I wasn't aware I was to be interrogated. I'm not obliged to answer your questions."

Like two lionesses stalking prey, they prowled around each other—one lithe and quick with cunning eyes and hands that curled like claws—the other impatient and strong-willed, with inner strength.

"My first instinct was to kill you," said McCall, only half-jokingly, "quietly and discreetly, of course. But the more I learned about you, the more . . . ah . . . curious I became. Here, at last, is a worthy rival, too beautiful and too complicated to simply destroy.

Alaina said, "Why would you feel threatened by me? You have authority and influence."

"I don't know what you're after, but I know you have power over Henry. That troubles me."

"You're troubled about what, exactly?"

"Perhaps I've expressed myself poorly. I don't think you appreciate Henry's significance."

"I understand more than you think," said Alaina.

"Perhaps."

Alaina Hepburn and Julie Ann McCall had different approaches when it came to dealing with men in general, and Henry Gallant in particular.

McCall said, "Kelsey Mitchell had a firm grip on Gallant before Neumann came along and upset that dynamic. Now you have him. Will you hold fast, or let him slip away?"

Alaina guessed that Henry would always have some tie to Kelsey. Some bonds do not break so easily. Is Kelsey still bound in her heart, as well as her marriage, to Neumann? What if she were free? Would Gallant seek her out again? Is he hers for the beckoning?

McCall wondered whether she had underestimated the younger woman. Intent on controlling Gallant, she had to be careful not to put Alaina on the defensive with too many personal questions. Alaina might lack sophistication, but there was a steadfastness about her.

Alaina broke the silence, "And what is your interest in Henry?"

"Oh, strictly professional, of course." The glib answer held little credence for either woman.

In fact, McCall considered Gallant of considerable importance to the fleet. But to her, he was a curiosity, a personal, and a professional opportunity. She had known him long enough to be both impressed and apprehensive about him. During their last mission, she had tried to seduce him, telling herself it was so she could better study him. But his resistance had surprised her, and she was disappointed that he hadn't succumbed to her advances.

The product of genetic engineering, McCall, had considerable skills in manipulation and deception. They had fostered her brilliant SIA career.

In contrast, Alaina was ever bold and direct, with a passion for being considered an equal in any venture. Her openness and honesty left her artless and unaffected. Although she might be aware of McCall's cunning and wile, she was helpless to counter it. Underneath her bravado, she was nervous, but as she talked, she became more confident.

"Henry Gallant is a good man," said Alaina earnestly.

Seething with sarcasm, McCall smirked, "So it's not his looks that attract you; it's his nobility of character?"

Alaina didn't respond.

McCall said, "OK, let's leave him out of this—for now. Let's just consider your intentions. From what I know of you, I'm concerned about your perspective. I want to . . . dissuade you from resisting certain developments that must occur for Elysium and its people. Otherwise, you will suffer severe consequences."

"All I've done is to stand up for the citizens."

"No, my dear, that's not all that you've done. You made it clear that you cannot be ignored, nor sidestepped, nor pushed aside. Whether you realize it or not, you've drawn a line in the sand. And when that line is crossed—which it will be—you will be trampled underfoot. You have no idea who and what you are dealing with. This is not about Henry. You are going against Anton Neumann and his father's NNR Corporation, the most powerful entity in the United Planets. You and this tiny town are defying the entire UP federation and the awesome power of NNR. There is nothing between you and utter destruction beyond what shelter Henry can provide, which won't be much, believe me."

Alaina felt the ugly truth of the words. Alaina sat down and twisted her hands together. "What can they do?"

"They've already started, you, foolish girl. They will remove your government, replacing it with a more pliable one of their choosing. Then they will take the planet's substantial resources for their own. Any resistance will be beaten down with financial pressure through the banks or intimidation."

"How can that be? I simply stated the facts, based on the treaty, which I have every reason to expect will be honored."

"And why should you expect that? You see, my dear, Neumann's father has bottled that treaty up in a senate committee. It'll never see the light of day, not even for a vote. He knows the incredible wealth this planet holds, and he intends to take the lion's share for himself through NNR. That's why they sent such a large contingent of new colonists. Those citizens will vote as he says, and the company will take over the mining and manufacturing facilities. You've betrayed your people by proposing opposition. By directly opposing NNR, you've made yourself a target—and unfortunately, you've exposed Gallant to a conflict of interest. He will try to help you, I'm sure, and in doing so, he too will feel Neumann's wrath."

"My position may be controversial, but Henry should not be placed in a vulnerable position."

"That may be what you wish, but it is not what will happen."

"Have I ruined everything? How can I repair this? How can I change the outcome?"

"I don't know whether that's still possible."

"Thank you for your opinion," Alaina retorted. "I will seek counsel from others."

"Yes, do that. One more thing: tread lightly. Do not lean on Henry. You may drag him down with you."

Satisfied she had said her piece, McCall turned and left the wardroom. But both women knew the controversy was far from over.

CHAPTER 20

Referendum

McCall's warning proved prophetic.

Alaina's enemies made sure the referendum was both painful and humiliating. News reports criticized her and others who spoke out. Nearly every day, Wolfe appeared on television. Her proposals for better cooperation between natives and the NNR settlers garnered little interest. But the worst was the personal attacks on her character—claims of immorality circulated without the slightest substantiation. Salacious gossip about her swept through the small community.

Gallant asked her, "How's the campaign going?"

She smiled wanly. "Not good. According to the polls."

"Wolfe is gaining support?"

"Yes, he has backing from his father's council-member cronies. Plus, several businessmen, who are benefiting from the NNR relationship.

Gallant said, "I know. I've seen some of the more disreputable ones."

Alaina blushed.

He said, "He's made frequent visits to the *Achilles*."

She scowled, "He's openly promoting his relationship with Neumann, claiming that NNR shares in the mining and manufacturing companies. Which will mean more jobs and financial gain for everyone. On the surface, there's an element of truth to it, but I know jobs are actually being redistributed away from the locals."

"Elections are supposed to be the expression of the will of the people, but I'm amazed at how easily the people can be led astray."

Aboard the *Achilles,* Gallant joined McCall in Neumann's stateroom. He took a seat on an antique French colonial chair, trying to be as casual about the anachronism as his two senior officers were.

Smiling broadly, Neumann asked, "How can I be of service?".

McCall said, "I'm sorry to interrupt your day. I know how busy you are with task force responsibilities. However, Commander Gallant has brought to my attention to some problems that I feel require your direction."

"I'm more than glad to lend a hand with resettling the new colonists. The settlers have made amazing progress on building homes and are opening new businesses and industries. I know the production at the mines is at an all-time high."

"Yes. The planet's economy is thriving."

Gallant shifted in his chair.

McCall said, "However, the politics on Elysium are heating up. The popular support seems to favor Cyrus Wolfe."

"Yes, so I've been informed. Hepburn brought that trouble on herself," said Neumann, waving his hand dismissively. "I welcome the news. Don't you?"

"I've found Hepburn to be intelligent, strong-willed, and determined. Although she may be difficult to work with, my opinion of Wolfe is that he is weak and ineffective. I believe he would be a poor partner going forward."

He leaned toward her and said with great deliberation, "I believe I can use Wolfe to my advantage."

Gallant looked uncomfortably at his two superior officers but remained silent.

"Pushing change on these people may ultimately prove to be counterproductive," McCall suggested.

"Is your conscience getting restive?" scoffed Neumann.

"It's a matter of strategic evaluation," replied McCall blandly.

"Wolfe is my man," said Neumann.

"I have no objection to a strategic move, but you are alienating a large faction of the population," said McCall. "The NNR settlers have hardly landed, and they are already clashing with the native population. The free genetic engineering clinics for future births in the community have caused particular unrest."

Neumann frowned. "Those are for the convenience of the population. Genetic engineering is not mandatory, just available for those who want it."

"Some seem to think mandatory requirements are in the wings."

"Nonsense. Hysteria."

Unable to remain quiet any longer, Gallant cut in, "We can remove that concern by issuing a policy statement that the clinics will remain voluntary."

There was silence in the room. Neumann sat perfectly still, his hands gripping the arms of his antique chair and his eyes blazing.

Finally, he managed to steady his voice. "Mr. Gallant, your heritage leads you astray on this issue."

Gallant bit his tongue so hard he tasted blood.

Neumann continued, "The forces at play here involve changes in the natural course of evolution. These things are complicated."

"Is that what you are? Complicated?" asked Gallant.

"The superiority of the genetically engineered is unquestioned."

Gallant snapped, "I question it."

"By removing genetic imperfections and adding enhancements, the genetically engineered are superior."

"Removing some imperfections does not necessarily produce perfection."

"Genetics has enhanced our people."

"Perhaps in some respects, it has. But nature's method of creating random variations offers opportunities for unanticipated improvements," argued Gallant.

"You consider yourself in that category?" McCall interjected.

"Perhaps."

Neumann said, "Planned with care, humanity's genetic modifications will lead to an improved and more uniform human species."

"That's your opinion," said Gallant. "But superiority planning would require a superior prototype to start with—one that will make no missteps. Otherwise, we risk directing the population into a blind alley."

"The human race is not heading into any blind alley, I assure you," said Neumann. "On the contrary, we are moving humanity into its era of highest achievement and success."

"Genetic prejudice is a powerful thing," said Gallant. "And it's never been a good thing, despite its many and varied forms throughout history."

"That's your opinion."

"Powerful men often believe that they can avoid the consequences of their action, but NNR's overreaching here will not end well," said Gallant.

"The universe does not have to conform to your personal code of honor. You are dangerously close to insubordination," seethed Neumann, standing with his fists clenched.

"Relax, Commander. We're all just having a friendly conversation here. Nothing more," said McCall.

The result of the referendum was no surprise. Though dismayed, Alaina accepted it.

Even as the people celebrated, Wolfe was busy drafting the details which the councilmembers quickly adopted. It nullified the previous arrangement with the United Planets in favor of a protected mining colony under the auspices of the NNR Corporation.

In private, Alaina muttered, "Damn Wolfe! Damn him!"

CHAPTER 21

The Mansion

The Wolfe family, for all its many scandals, was highly regarded, as much for its wealth and power as for its accomplishments. Originally built by Cyrus Wolfe Sr., the mansion was lavish by any standard, but especially imposing compared to the rest of Halo's homes. A sweeping stairway climbed past a marble fireplace and granite tile paved the entryway.

Tonight, music from a grand piano filled the elegant ballroom, an impeccable ebony and glass room. Guests clustered around as the pianist played a classical piece, then a contemporary one, eliciting enthusiastic applause. The music touched something fundamental in their spirit as they celebrated Cyrus Wolf's referendum victory.

Gallant was surprised to receive an invitation to the festivities. As far as he knew, none of Wolfe's circle considered him worthy of attention, or even recognition. The invitation said the evening would be an opportunity for everyone to meet Wolfe. He hoped there would be a chance to talk freely with both Wolfe and Neumann about the future of Elysium.

When he asked Alaina to attend the event with him, she said, "No, Henry. Go if you like, but I shan't. I'm not their sort, and it is not my occasion."

Thus, Gallant found himself standing unaccompanied in the crowded ballroom, surrounded by the colony's elite society. The garden's perfume filled the warm evening air, mingling among the men and women in their finery. There were several couples dancing.

"Commander Gallant, I'm so glad to see you. What do you make of the settlement arrangement?" asked Councilman Rothschild.

"Must you talk business?" asked his wife with a sigh.

Rothschild set little store on fashion, but his wife advanced their social status by scrupulously observing the latest trends. She wore a flowered dress of the finest synthetic silk laced with gold embroidery. An unsuitable dress for traveling from Earth to another planet, it set a stunning standard for the current crowd. She was much younger than her husband— pretty, happy, and of a merry disposition, tending to laugh over trivialities. Though the gossips whispered that she lacked judgment, Rothschild rarely denied her anything.

"Business?" he repeated. In truth, he did prefer

business over social graces. He had lost his temperament for polite conversation many years ago, but to placate his wife, he gave a weak smile, nodded, and followed her meekly toward the dance floor.

Gallant nodded in return. He threaded his way between the chatting couples and the rustling dresses, wandering aimlessly. To his great surprise, Alaina suddenly appeared in the doorway.

Her entrance hushed the room. Perhaps the stunned silence was due to her dramatic fall from grace, but it could as easily have been an acknowledgment of her beauty. She too wore a magnificent gown, but one that had come from Elysium's rudimentary clothing industry.

Breathless, Gallant watched her sweep through the room. He stepped forward to escort her through the crowd, but before he took two steps, Liam appeared out of nowhere and claimed her.

"So, this is the rabble-rouser," said Mrs. Rothschild. "I don't see why there was so much fuss about her."

"Have another drink, dear," said her husband, gawking at Alaina.

Gallant hovered in the background until Liam left Alaina alone, probably to get them drinks. He stepped up and touched her arm.

"You're very persistent, Henry," she said.

"Only because you're very stubborn," he smiled.

"I hope you find what you're looking for," she said as if he were merely passing by.

"What if I've already found it?"

She was unreadable; he couldn't tell what she was thinking. Still, she let him lead her to a table and didn't object when he pulled his chair closer.

He was proud of Alaina's aplomb and quiet dignity in such an awkward situation. She hummed and sang softly to herself, along with the music.

She leaned closer, and Gallant wrapped his arm around her shoulder. As she pressed close to him, he felt her heart beating, felt her warm breath on his neck. Her body was familiar to him, yet somehow distant and removed in this time and place.

I'm happy to be with her. Nothing else matters.

Gallant pushed his emotions away and tried to talk bravely about the future. He wanted to explain his next mission and longed to ask her to wait for him. But he couldn't find the right words.

They went for a walk on the veranda, and the moonlight glistened on her face.

"Henry, when do you have to leave?"

"Soon."

She cast her eyes down and said nothing.

"I will not fail. Trust in that."

"The one thing I need to hear is the one thing you cannot say."

"What do you need to hear?"

"That I come first."

Gallant remained silent.

"Henry," she said. "Look at me."

He turned and cupped her face in his hands, his eyes probing hers.

She stepped up and held him close. He felt her relax in his embrace, then tense again, and she put her hands on his chest and pushed him away.

"Can I walk you home?" he asked.

"No. I need to clear my head."

"All right. If that's what you need."

He didn't want to pressure her. She would choose her own time and place to make her needs known to him. As she walked away, Liam emerged from the ballroom, and Alaina laughed and reached for his hand.

He watched them leave together.

CHAPTER 22

Unrest

The gently rolling hills of New Kauai often fell off into hollows wedged between high bordering mountain ridges. Narrow stone-paved roads worked their way up the many creek beds. They got narrower and more difficult to navigate as they climbed the ridges. A typical hollow had several houses set on the hillside overlooking the valley of another hollow. This rich soil supported family farms on which a variety of grain crops, fruits, and vegetables were grown. The fields held wheat and oats, as well as barley, a portion of which was to be stored to feed the domestic animals. Orchards and vineyards peppered the areas where dairy farmers raised livestock and fowl.

Unfortunately, the planet's normal abundance had suffered a setback due to excessive rainfall, followed by an early frost. The farmers were anxious about their yields. It was harvest time, and the crops were growing ripe for the picking. They merely lacking the labor force to collect them. The mills and granaries were also waiting to be staffed. The schools were set to let out early so that the farmer's children could help. Unfortunately, many family farmers were forced to labor in the mines and manufacturing facilities to support NNR.

The mining mineral deposits were being exploited to the maximum. In the short time that the mines had been operating, they had gathered vast quantities of ore. The workers mined the backside of the lode. They found that the ore-bearing rock existed in great mass and extended several hundred meters into the volcano wall. Not everyone was excited by the news—the drafted farmers were anxious to get on with the harvest. Following Neumann's demands, Wolfe gave priority to the production of the weapons systems. This required the farmers to remain in the mines—the farmers would have to stay on the job and watch their crops rot.

Concerned about the slow production of key parts, Gallant rode an elevator down a narrow shaft on the ocean side of the Brobdingnag Volcano. At the bottom of the shaft, he climbed down ladders and over rock ledges into the deepest part of the mine. Fumes of dust hung in the air, making each breath of grime-laden air difficult. When he reached the bottom, Gallant was gravely disappointed. Everything was in disrepair. There were loose rocks to be moved from the mouth of the mine, support beams in weakened states, and airflow regulators broke or in disorder. He knew he would have his work cut out for him reestablishing discipline to resume safe operations.

He arranged a meeting with Treadwell and several of his foremen at a local tavern that catered to the native population.

Treadwell spoke to his men, "Remember, I'll do the talking."

They nodded all around, not wanting their dissatisfaction to get lost in some hyperbolic tangent. "You do all the talking. We'd rather just listen."

They all turned and faced Gallant. Their faces were grim.

Gallant asked, "I appreciate the efforts you've made to produce the specialized parts *Warrior* needs. However, there are still a number of critical items remaining that must be pushed on the schedule. I trust you're making progress upgrading the robotic equipment to boost output?"

"You gotta be jokin'," said Treadwell.

"Is there a problem I can help with?"

"Naught to do."

"I'm disappointed to hear that."

Treadwell downed his ale, wiped his mouth with the back of his hand, and said, "I'm glad you've come. We've talked among ourselves, and now we want to be heard. First, though, we need to know that everything said here stays in confidence."

"Of course, I will respect your confidence."

"All right, then."

Gallant said, "While the Warrior has received

our essential materials, I'm concerned about the remaining critical parts."

Treadwell said, "That's your concern, and as should be. But we've concerns, as well."

The older man rubbed his chin and furrowed his brow. He said, "On behalf of NNR, Rothschild has gained a majority share of Elysium's mining and manufacturing."

Gallant raised his brows in surprise.

"That's right, Commander. Instead of improving our existing industry, as promised, NNR is building new factories that use high-tech robotics. On top of that, our wages have been cut drastically, and will be again before this is over."

"I see," said Gallant.

One of the foremen said, "This arrangement is a cancer. We need to cut it out."

Another said, "Cut it? We should shoot it."

A third worried, "But what will happen to our workers?"

The second said, "We've been here for twenty years, making our living from this planet. We'll manage to survive. But we need to get rid of these NNR parasites."

The third said, "I don't even want to go in the mines anymore. They're too dangerous!"

Treadwell interrupted, "Now, didn't we agree to let me do the talkin'?"

The foremen fell silent, fidgeting uncomfortably.

Treadwell went on, "The working arrangements with the NNR people are unsatisfactory. If you haven't already guessed, we need to restructure our business arrangement."

Gallant asked, "Restructure? In what way?"

"We want to split the entire mining and manufacturing work in two. One to be run for the natives, the other is owned by NNR. That way, we can be our own masters, like it was before. We can set the work to suit ourselves and pay ourselves a living wage."

"You want to compete directly against NNR? Is that wise?" asked Gallant.

"May not be wise, but it's necessary. NNR controls everything, and they are driving us out altogether. We get less pay, dangerous job assignments, and bad working hours and conditions. We have no say and none of the training on the high-tech equipment."

"That is troubling."

"If we band together, we can set our own work and pay. We have saved some money, and most of our workers are ready to walk away from NNR."

"What about the mining leases from Halo?"

"That's the other shoe that hasn't dropped. Wolfe keeps stalling us and gives all the deals to NNR. We need to start something moving, and soon, or we'll have no rights left at all."

"What can I do to help?"

"Can you speak to Commander Neumann about NNR and the new settlers?"

"Sure, but I don't know if that will change anything."

Just a few weeks earlier, Halo had been a thriving, happy community. Now crowds grew, from a few dozen to several thousand in just a few hours. The original colonists of Elysium gathered in Freedom Park to express their anger and frustration. The disenfranchisement resulted from Wolfe's policies and NNR Corporation's restrictions. The disparities in work and pay between the natives and the new arrivals had stirred the unrest. Burgeoning distrust over genetic engineering threatened to ignite a dangerous fuse. Genetic engineering of an embryo was not mandatory, but those who did not want it faced onerous restrictions and requirements.

Children were running and playing in the park while several shadowy figures were gathering in a corner under a stand of trees at the far end. The squealing sounds of the young ones resounded in the distance as the figures quietly exchanged looks and information.

The protestors began marching in an organized fashion along a narrow side street toward the outskirts of town. Each step they took was marked by furtive glances over their shoulders. Soon the playful squeals diminished in the distance.

Fear and helplessness breed desperate men, and desperation produces nothing good. Over the next week, there were disruptions in the mines. Several men were arrested for violence and destroying government property and placed on trial.

Although Neumann wanted to hold the trial aboard the *Achilles*, he relented. It took place in Halo's town hall—a concession intended to soothe hurt feelings.

The prosecutor asked, "William Treadwell, are you the engineering supervisor at the Brobdingnag mine?"

"Well, some say, I am, and some say, I ain't." Treadwell glanced around his chair as if looking for someplace to spit, but seeing none, he continued to chew.

"Mr. Treadwell, are you the appointed engineer for the mine, or not?"

"I'm the engineer for the mine, but I volunteered to serve without pay. I was not appointed."

"Then I take it the two defendants who pleaded guilty to malicious mischief and have been sentenced accordingly, obey your orders. Is that correct?"

"Can't say that it is, can't say it isn't."

"Do they work for you at the mine?"

"Yes."

"Then it follows they obey your orders, doesn't it?"

"Sometimes they do, sometimes they don't."

The prosecutor continued for fifteen minutes before he finally reached his exasperation point. He conceded that he wouldn't get anything specific enough from Treadwell to constitute an admission. He sat down, wiping the sweat from his face.

The defense attorney rose and asked a single

question. "Mr. Treadwell, did you order the other two defendants to commit any criminal acts?"

"Nope."

"That's all. You may return to your seat."

Till now, Gallant had been unable to be more than a spectator, but it was critical to get the attention of the court.

He said, "If I may ask for the indulgence of the court, I would like to offer a character reference for this man for I know him from his work at the mines."

"Shouldn't your time be better spent aboard the *Warrior* seeing to repairs?" Neumann's grim mouth curved sourly.

"I have men working diligently on that, sir. I felt I was needed here."

Neumann cast a stern look on him, very much unhappy with the exchange.

Gallant said, "Gentlemen, on the evidence, this man has committed some unacceptable acts, but his intention was as a protestor. He wanted to draw attention to a grievous wrong, not to be a disloyal citizen and certainly not as an advocate for violence or malicious damage."

"Stop right there, Gallant. You are not here to make a political statement or to instigate a grievance committee. State your knowledge of his man's behavior as you know it and conclude with that."

Gallant said, "I am personally aware of his good character and efforts on our behalf. This despite his farm suffering a complete loss of crops leaving his family in dire straits. I ask the court to consider these facts."

"This man's misfortunes are no excuse for vandalizing government property in a time of war. He's lucky the case for treason was too weak to pursue farther, though a case could still be made for that."

Gallant said, "I recommend leniency."

"You may well feel that way. But the decision rests with this court, and considering the lawless nature of the acts involved, I am not so inclined," said Neumann, thrusting out his jaw.

There was a murmur in the court.

Neumann said, "The prisoner is sentenced to two years imprisonment."

Sounds of dissent could be heard while Neumann rapped the table with his gavel.

CHAPTER 23

Shakedown Cruise

"Welcome aboard, Commander," said Gallant, greeting Neumann and his surprise inspection team.

Neumann stepped through the hatch, gave a curt nod in Gallant's direction, and proceeded straight to the *Warrior's* bridge. His gait was stiff and proper, as unyielding as his judgment. He stepped carefully around the repair sites he passed, intent on keeping his polished shoes and pressed uniform, untarnished.

His entourage of engineers and technicians remained behind, uncertain of the protocol. His personal escort of two marines also remained at the hatch.

As Neumann disappeared down the corridor, Gallant turned to Roberts. "XO, have personnel escort the review teams to the requested areas to conduct their inspections and test procedures. I will join Commander Neumann on the bridge and monitor your progress from there."

"Aye aye, Skipper."

With his usual efficiency, Roberts gave the inspection team a report on the ship's repair status and equipment needs. He provided a schedule for the impending shakedown cruise.

Chief Howard greeted the teams with a brisk, "Welcome to the *Warrior*! We're glad to have your help and expertise. We can use all the helping hands and experienced eyes we can get." He smiled and pumped the hand of a senior chief, who had once been a shipmate of his.

Sitting in the *Warrior's* command chair, Neumann flipped through viewscreens. He said pointedly, "You're behind schedule."

Gallant replied, "We're a few days behind, but I'm hopeful we can make that up. We're still waiting for some of the redesigned replacement parts from Elysium's facilities. I expect to meet our scheduled deployment."

Neumann looked doubtful. "Elysium's mining and manufacturing efforts are proving troublesome. The native population is unruly and less productive than the new settlers. Their engineering supervisor, Treadwell, has been a thorn in my side."

Gallant frowned.

"We're fighting a war with the Titans," Neumann's jaw tightened as he added, "Wolfe told me that Treadwell was agitating the workers. I expect the workers to be more compliant. If not, he'll pay."

Gallant said, "Part of the problem in productivity is the division of labor and equipment. NNR personnel have kept all the new robotic equipment for their own use and haven't trained the natives on it."

"Are you blaming their performance on their tools?"

"Not just that. NNR has taken over the most lucrative mines and used that material to build new plants and factories. They do not help our existing ones."

"So, you think investing in plants and equipment for massively better industrial production is a mistake?"

"Of course, not. That's a necessary long-term goal. But …."

"Or that manufacturing missiles and satellites for the defense of Elysium should be a low priority?"

"Again, no. But the result is a divided workforce that skews the delivery schedule away from the *Warrior's* needs."

"Personally, I'm pleased with the progress the new colonists. They have homes and their own industrial base. It raises the standard for all of Elysium. I hope to see this planet thrive over the next years, far beyond the modest gains of the original population.

Gallant looked askance at Neumann. He said, "The people of Elysium started out as prisoners of the Titans. They fought their way free and built this tiny community. With virtually no equipment or resources, they made a home. They are a hardy and innovative people. I believe they've accomplished a great deal."

Neumann's eyes bored into Gallant as if taking his measure. He said, "Your sympathy for the locals is affecting your judgment. You're using them as an excuse for the lax performance of your duties. Further, I believe your involvement with that Hepburn woman is clouding your judgment. I expect you to meet your deployment commitment, or I will be forced to take action."

"With your permission, sir, I'll go to engineering to observe the testing?" asked Gallant, grinding his teeth.

"Granted."

They didn't speak to each other for the rest of the day. Gallant avoided his superior's gaze.
He focused all his energy on the exhaustive inspections and testing throughout the ship.

The *Warrior* received a deficient grade for failure to meet the repair standards Neumann set. Gallant received a personal reprimand for lax performance in his personnel file.

Before leaving, Neumann said to Gallant, "Roberts should be qualified for an independent command, by now. Haven't you been training him?"

Gallant furrowed his brow and clenched his jaw. He said, "Yes, of course. I've been conducting training, and he has completed his qualifications book. The preliminary exams were administered by the ship's AI..."

"Then what's the holdup?" Neumann's face relaxed into an insolent expression. He stood up from his chair and crossed the few steps to come close to Gallant's face.

Gallant didn't get so far as opening his mouth before, Neumann continued, "I assumed you would recommend him? Does he lack the character or skill? If so, then he shouldn't remain as XO. That's a position where he would be responsible for replacing you if you fell in battle."

Gallant remained silent and stood perfectly straight under Neumann's glare. He started, "I . . . uh . . . No, he doesn't lack . . ." Then he said firmly, "Yes, I'm prepared to recommend that he take his final command exam. It's just that all the work on ship repairs, deployment preparation, plus the expedited timetable have overloaded our . . ."

Unfazed, Neumann said, "Very well, I will arrange for an exam team of three captains to be ready to accompany you on shakedown. He can demonstrate his abilities then. Dismissed."

Gallant was caught short, baffled by the demand, as if he were being called to heel, more like a threat than a duty. He wondered why Neumann was anxious to have his XO qualify for command. His head was spinning with numerous arguments rattling inside. He considered for a moment, whether he really believed that Roberts was ready for command.

Yes. He is.

Gallant watched as the last members of the surprise inspection team left with Neumann. Roberts stood beside him as he said, "John, I'm recommending you for command."

Roberts looked startled, then pleased. He said, "Of course, after this mission, you'll be up for a major promotion, and they probably want me to step up. Great."

Gallant didn't think that was Neumann's thinking, but it was a possibility. "Maybe you're right, John, but don't discuss this with anyone else. I've already recommended you to Captain Neumann, and he is arranging an examination team to board *Warrior* during our shakedown. You'll handle the ship and the drills for the dual purpose of qualifying the ship and yourself at the same time."

"Wow! That's quick. And complicated."

"There isn't any other time that's practical."

"I guess not."

"Will you be ready?"

"I'll have to be."

"I'll see that you get as much time as possible for any last-minute studies while we finish the remaining repairs. Hopefully, the worst crunch is over."

To meet their schedule, a veritable army of military and civilian workers crawled over, under, and through the ship. The acrid smell of welding, the din of construction tools, and the clamor of workers never ceased.

Soon the *Warrior* looked as if she had been put back together, though she lacked the spit and polish that they would later give her. She was mechanically complete, but definitely not the thing of beauty she had once been. Her decks were covered with a tarp and discarded wiring and miscellaneous parts. The unkempt appearance belied her state of readiness. All systems were functioning within acceptable parameters.

Three captains arrived just in time for departure and crowded onto the bridge as Gallant entered, smiling pleasantly.

Roberts said, "Good morning, Skipper. All preparations for getting underway have been completed. Engines are in hot standby."

"Good morning. Thank you, XO. Has the sailing list been transmitted to the flagship?"

"Yes, sir." Gallant noted that the list was considerably shorter than when he first took command. The sailing list contained the IDs and pertinent information of those embarked. In case the ship was lost, next of kin could be notified.

"Maneuvering watch is set. All stations report manned and ready, sir," said Chief Howard.

"Mr. Roberts, you have the bridge and the conn. Proceed with the shakedown cruise."

"Aye aye, sir," said Roberts. He stepped up to the command deck and took the command seat vacated by his captain. The examination members were skulking along the back of the bridge, trying to keep out of the way.

Roberts ordered, "Engineering, bridge; standby to answer all bells."

"Bridge, engineering; ready to answer all bells,

sir," came the response.

"Helmsman, set course to take the *Warrior* out of orbit, ahead one third."

"Aye aye, sir."

The helmsman rang up the increased acceleration on the engineering console.

Gallant felt there was no reason for Roberts to 'sweat' getting underway. He had done that often enough. The hard choices would come later, but for now, Gallant had to let Roberts act as captain. Gallant could only step in if the safety of the ship was in jeopardy. Of course, if he did have to take command, then that would automatically fail Roberts.

Roberts ordered, "Helm, set course to our designated operating area."

The *Warrior* was on her way.

The shakedown drills and tests were to be conducted in a portion of space about fifty million kilometers from Elysium.

The engineering drills started with driving the engine to maximum acceleration. Drills simulated system failures, and the crew responded.

A test profile and long list of exercises to stretch the ship's operating envelop were conducted to assure she could meet her mission.

The crew was doing its best to support their XO, but there was still a great deal of chaos from equipment testing and final adjustments.

Gallant watched with great anticipation each evolution and every order Roberts issued.

There were three key pieces of equipment that

needed testing: first, the sublight engines required maneuvering drills; second, the cloaking system needed evaluation; and third, weapons required target practice.

The drills began. It was a tough grind keeping up a quick tempo. A lot of work went into the weapon systems and the stealth capability, both of which were critical for the *Warrior's* mission.

The operational readiness inspection was completed as the last step in the shakedown. A feeling of tension ran throughout the ship. Gallant read over the examiner's critique of the cruise. He read every line and evaluated every nuance. Then they finally returned to port and fixed any last-minute items. They topped off supplies, cleaned the ship and were ready to depart for its mission.

Maneuvers and emergency procedures were tested at a grueling pace. A haggard Roberts trudged onto the bridge on the third day. As part of his qualifications, he was ordered to make a mock attack on one of the UP destroyers.

Afterward, it was clear that *Warrior* was ready to fight again—and she was restless to get on with her mission. So, the three-captain exam team qualified Roberts for command. It remained a mystery when an opportunity for his own ship might occur.

"Congratulations," Gallant said, shaking Roberts' hand.

CHAPTER 24

Fidelity

Seated at the wardroom table across from Gallant, Commander McCall looked particularly sharp in her freshly pressed service dress blue uniform. Compared to her, he felt shabby in his working blues, although the officers around him were similarly attired. They were all laughing and enjoying a slightly ribald story McCall had just told.

He was on the verge of reminding them of the proper decorum for the wardroom when he changed his mind. Instead, he sat silently, preoccupied, looking only at the meal before him. After a time, he grew tired of his petty revenge and observed McCall making polite conversation with Roberts. She was asking him about an experience he'd had as a midshipman, though Gallant knew for sure he had described that event to her at least once before.

The conversation around the table grew more genial and animated as various officers were all too willing regaled the gathering with tall tales of their academy days. Before long, he joined in, laughing as gaily as any of the others. Not until the dinner ended did the merriment cease.

As the others finished their meals and left to return to duty, almost against his will, he found himself enjoying a personal conversation with McCall. They talked of trivialities and petty gripes for several minutes, and Gallant wondered, whether after their long months of strife, they might have formed a bond. He dismissed the thought, assuming the anomaly would dissipate once they were assigned new missions.

He was feeling relaxed and open when McCall suddenly asked, "Have you been to see Neumann?"

"I've not seen him," he replied. "Our quarrel is not the sort likely to be made up."

"Not ever?"

"Ours is an enduring and private feud, one that must play out between the two of us. For the sake of your career, you'd do well to stay out of the hostilities."

"I've never yet done that," she said with a strained look.

"There's something I should tell you."

"Is it in the past?"

"Yes."

"Then forget about it. I don't need to hear it," said McCall.

He grew quiet. The good cheer of the dinner had passed.

McCall's demeanor shifted abruptly, her friendly attitude disappearing like a chameleon changing color.

She said, "He intends to bring charges against you. I spent hours talking to him about why that might not be appropriate."

"He's concerned about my superintelligence abilities?"

"Yes."

"You share those concerns?"

"No."

He asked, "What was his reaction to my report?"

"Rather curious. He was more unsettled about your opinion on the Titan's experiments with genetic engineering than your superintelligence experiences."

Gallant remained silent.

"He railed against your assessment that their manipulation of the genetic pool diverted their natural evolution toward inferiority rather than superiority."

"He didn't agree with my conclusions?"

"Hardly."

"What about you?"

"I confess, I'm troubled by the implication that genetic engineering took the Titans down a dead-end path. But that doesn't mean that the United Planets would make the same mistake."

Gallant said, "I've seen the result of the Titans' genetic engineering face to face. It's not pretty. There are hatcheries dedicated to producing various classes who are programmed into their lives—no creativity or diversity, no options, no choices in their life. That's not the path I want for humanity, locked in DNA handcuffs. Instead of a path to superintelligence, I see genetic engineering as a path to super-disaster."

She was silent for a moment, then said softly, "It's not up to you to make those decisions."

"And yet Neumann is about to make genetic engineering mandatory on Elysium. It's not even mandatory on Earth. Don't you think that's dangerous?"

McCall looked doubtful.

Gallant asked, "I believe we can defeat the Titans by using their own network against them."

She didn't reply.

"Will there be another mission to Gliese?" he persisted.

She said, "It will be up to Admiral Collingsworth if anyone goes back to Gliese."

"You're still worried about my fidelity?"

She didn't have to answer. Her expression answered the question all too clearly.

He looked at her eyes—bright, intense, searching eyes. Once he had thought he could read their expression, but now he knew they were well-trained practitioners of deception and manipulation—hard, disingenuous, untrusting black orbs.

CHAPTER 25

Betrothal

The wind picked up as the sunset; a brief gust blew grit into Gallant's face as he made his way toward the center of town. The walkway, usually so well-tended, was strewn with debris. He noticed several people peering at him from their windows as he passed. One couple, both gaunt and care-worn, stopped in the street to stare at him.

"Your pardon, sir," said the wife. "You look familiar. In fact, I think you're the officer who saved us. Aren't you?"

She wore a threadbare dress to match her husband's faded and torn miner's coveralls. Gallant had no doubt they were original Elysium inhabitants, hardy people who had struggled to build their community.

"Yes, you're the one, aren't you?" asked the husband. "I have a good memory for faces. I saw you on the newscast."

"Commander Gallant, captain of the *Warrior*," he acknowledged with a curt bow of his head.

The couple nodded and smiled.

"Ah, yes, Mr. Gallant. It's good to see you walking about town."

Gallant nodded his thanks and continued, leaving them behind as he quickened the pace toward his destination. Finally, he reached the fork that headed toward the center of town, but he veered toward the rustic section of town—where Alaina lived.

The Hepburn house beckoned him, bright and cheery. His arrival coincided with dinner time, but that couldn't be helped. He didn't have a lot of time to say his farewells before leaving on his mission.

At the entrance, the door computer recognized him and granted him access.

"Do you wish to be announced, Lieutenant Commander Henry Gallant?" asked the automated voice.

"I'll announce myself, thank you."

As he walked from the foyer into the living room, he heard a good deal of chatter from the dining room, but he didn't recognize the older women and men. However, he did recognize Liam and Alaina sitting amongst the rather large gathering. The dining table was stacked with many dishes of poultry, fish, and vegetables, leaving a wafting aroma of delicious flavors.

"Dear, don't you think she should eat more?" said the oldest woman, giving Alaina a critical look. "She's as skinny as a rail."

"I agree," the man next to her nodded. "A little flesh is healthy on a strong young woman."

The crowd roared with laughter.

"Liam, coax her to eat more."

"She's perfect just the way she is," said Liam, fixing his eyes on Alaina.

Gallant glanced at the handsome dark-haired young man with a charming smile.

"Yes, yes." The crowd echoed enthusiastically.

"What was that? Is someone at the door?" asked one of the men.

"Are we expecting more company?" asked the old woman glancing at the entrance.

All eyes turned toward Gallant, who felt exposed to his eavesdropping. Each member of the group uttered a mild exclamation of surprise.

"My goodness!" explained the old woman.

"Who . . .?" asked the old man.

Gallant emerged from the shadows and stepped into the room. A window curtain fluttered, and the sunlight exposed him clearly for the first time.

Alaina and Liam rose. The others followed suit.

The old man scratched his forehead while the old woman said, "Who's there? Who is that?"

Gallant hadn't intended on intruding on an on-going party, but he was now in their midst and could not withdraw.

The first to recover his wits was Liam, who approached Gallant and said, "Henry, Henry, how good to see you. We had no idea you would come tonight."

He turned to the company and explained, "This

is Henry Gallant, the brave officer who fought the Titans." There was a general murmur of appreciation. Then turning to Henry again, he said, "This is my family and some guests."

He then proceeded to introduce his mother, father, and three sisters, followed by a clergyman and a member of the town council. He spoke so quickly that Gallant didn't get all the names.

The elderly couple was Liam's mother, a large woman, and his father, a big bear of a man. The councilman was the shorter of the two outsiders. He was in his early sixties with bowed legs and a hoarse, throaty voice.

"So, you're here, and we're glad to have you," said the councilman.

"Are you well, Henry?" asked Alaina after a moment.

"I'm fine now that I am here with you," he said, awkwardly. And "awkward" was the correct word because his last utterance seemed to cause a stir in the room and a bit of chattering that he couldn't quite make out.

Alaina's cheeks flushed a vivid ruby.

"Well, welcome to our gathering, Commander," said the clergyman.

Gallant nodded.

"Please join us," said Liam's mother. "Let me get you a plate." She busied herself at the table while Liam's father put his arm around Gallant's shoulder and guided him to a chair at the middle of the table. Alaina sat back down at the head, eyes on her lap, with Liam next to her.

"No, that's not necessary. I have business to attend to. I just stopped here on my way to say ... well to see... I just wanted to let Alaina know ..."

Everyone started to speak at once, and there was confusion for a moment.

Then Liam's mother said, "Alaina would you..."

Chatter drowned out the rest of her request.

"It's not an easy time ..."

"Lot's happening on Elysium ..."

Out of politeness, Gallant forced down a few swallows of food despite his lack of appetite. He said, "I've interrupted a party. Is it a celebration?"

The gathering fell silent.

"Well, actually," said Liam. "I ... err, the circumstances are ..."

His was not an easy face to read, and the situation was confusing for Gallant.

"This is a very special family celebration," said Liam's mother. "Liam is to be married."

"Married?" Gallant asked. "That's wonderful. To whom ...?"

"Why to Alaina, of course," laughed the old woman.

Gallant was sure she said more, but he stopped listening. He focused his stare on Alaina.

The woman continued, "We have been hoping for this wonderful announcement since they were children. They were always together. Two peas in a pod, as it were."

The following silence almost smothered Gallant.

Liam stood up once more.

Alaina looked down at the table.

"We're all very happy to see this union," said Liam's father. "I'm sure you'll join us in a toast to the happy couple."

"Of course," said Gallant.

"A toast to the happy couple," said Liam's father raising his glass high.

They toasted and drank quickly.

In the silence that followed, Gallant couldn't take his eyes off Alaina, though she never looked at him.

Gallant pushed back his chair. "I hope my mistimed arrival hasn't disturbed your good evening."

"Of course not," replied Liam's mother.

"I merely wanted to take my leave. The *Warrior* is deploying on a mission, and we'll be gone for some time."

He turned and walked blindly out of the room and toward the door. Before he reached it, Alaina appeared and grabbed his arm.

He swung around to face her. They stood no more than a half meter apart.

She wavered, her anxious eyes searching his face. "Henry don't look at me that way. You're the one who's leaving, facing untold dangers for who knows how long, leaving me behind yet again in complete uncertainty."

"I know I was gone a long time before. I had no

choice. But I came back then, and I'll come back from this mission." Then he added, "I want you to stop seeing Liam."

"I can't. I won't. You have no right to ask that of me."

"But nothing's settled? You haven't set a date for a wedding? Not yet?"

"No."

"Then I still have my chance. Will you wait until I return?"

"Can you offer me something more to hope for?"

He winced, studying her face.

"Please wait," he pleaded, taking her hand.

"No. You're too late. I won't change my mind. I understand your desire, your passion for me, but that's not enough for a lifetime commitment. I need stability and solidity, not a series of visits from an occasional lover."

She pulled her hand away. "I intend to marry Liam."

The thought of losing her struck him like a physical blow. He grasped her arm, and without meaning to, squeezed.

"Don't, Henry, you're hurting me. I'll make my own decisions."

"Why are you marrying Liam?"

"I love him."

"No. You don't—you love me."

"I did once, but I'm terribly sentimental. I fall in love too easily," she said. "I can't live half a life,

Henry. You're gone more than you're here. I want someone who will come home every day and put his arms around me and love me. I don't want an absent, or a dead, hero!"

Gallant said, "I don't want to be a hero, dead or otherwise. I want to be the man who comes home every day and puts his arms around you and loves you." He hesitated before adding, "But there's a war. An enemy is killing our people—your people, my people, all of us."

She reached out and touched his cheek. "War has made you noble and self-sacrificing. Why must you be so fierce?"

"I don't revere war. I don't believe in building monuments to it. But I do understand when it's necessary to fight."

Alaina looked troubled. "I can't live with always wondering where you are, if you're fighting in some far-off place, perhaps already dead—just a body floating in space."

"Every man and woman can find the courage to be heroic for some moment—when they or their loved ones are threatened. But those who face danger for the sake of others are our real heroes." He paused, fighting to steady his voice. "I'm not a hero, but I knew a hero once, a young man named Michael Gabriel. He went into harm's way and died, but his sacrifice saved many lives." He swallowed hard before adding, "I've got a job to do, a necessary one for all our sakes, and I won't shirk it."

"Is that what you're fighting for—other

people?"

He touched her arm. "I'm fighting for you—and a home and our people."

Tears welled up into her eyes and fell down her cheeks.

Gallant said, "It's not just the two of us. This war is not a choice. It comes against our will—by an enemy who has only one demand—that we cease to exist." He paused. "I wish I could just walk away and let it be someone else's burden, let others do the fighting for us. But I have a part to play in this war— perhaps an important part—and I can't just think of myself, or even you."

"Then go, Henry. Go! But don't look back because I won't be there." She wiped her tears away. "I've had my romantic dreams, and for a while, you were part of them. But not anymore. I don't regret having loved you, but I can't go on loving you."

His head drooping, he said, "I'll go, but I won't give up."

Alaina reached up and brushed a lock of hair off his forehead. "Don't look so sad, Henry. Not everyone can have their heart's desire."

She drew a breath and shrugged as if she were slipping a coat off her shoulders. "I must be practical in my future. Liam will make me a good husband. I'll be happy with him."

Just then, Liam stepped into the foyer.

Gallant wasn't sure how much the man had overheard. He said, "You can't blame me for trying to hold on to her."

Liam said, "No. And you can't blame me for refusing to give her up."

Alaina said, "Henry, you have to leave." She added more forcibly, "Go! Do your duty! Forget me."

Her words stung. "Alaina . . . ."

The look on his face softened her heart. She gave a small smile and kissed him gently on the cheek.

As she turned and walked away with Liam by her side, she said a hushed, "Goodbye, Henry."

Gallant whispered back, "Goodbye, my love."

But he knew he would see her again. He couldn't go on living without seeing her again.

CHAPTER 26

Cruisers

J ust after four bells into the morning watch, Lieutenant Commander Henry Gallant strode onto the
bridge of the Warrior. His second in command,
Lieutenant John Roberts, was already discussing the
coming evolution with the OOD. The abrupt change
of mission had caused significant changes to the ship's
routine—requiring the XO's attention.

Gallant occupied his command chair during
the ship's evolution. The crew had become accustomed to his remaining silent, lost in thought until
something specific required his attention.

"We've reached the Tau Ceti asteroid belt, sir,"
reported the sensor tech in an enthusiastic voice.

Excitement rippled over the bridge in anticipation of the coming operation.

Gallant was also eager but made every effort to
appear nonchalant, ordering simply, "Helm, come to
course 180 mark 2."

"Aye aye, sir."

"Steady on course 180 mark 2, sir."

"Very well. Ahead standard."

"Aye aye, sir," said the helmsman, signaled the sub-light reactors.

The OOD reported, "Sir, we're twenty light-hours from the target area."

"Very well," said Gallant.

The OOD said, "Request permission to conduct a long-range scan, sir."

"Granted," said Gallant. He did a quick calculation on the limits of long-range scans. He concluded that they would get meaningful results only on the fifth planet—a gas giant with numerous volcanic methane moons.

"I'm getting indications of several bases and satellites near the fifth planet's moons," reported the sensor tech. A few minutes, later he added, "Sir, I'm detecting ships near the largest moon."

Gallant muttered, "Send a sighting report to the *Achilles*."

Neumann was in the *Achilles* with four escort destroyers ten light-hours behind the *Warrior*.

"Recommend entering stealth mode and investigating, Skipper," said Roberts. "The Titans may have received reinforcements while we were away."

He ordered, "Enter stealth mode. Set course for the fifth planet."

"Aye aye, sir," said the OOD.

A few minutes later, Roberts said, "Our scans reveal four Titan cruisers are orbiting the largest moon of the fifth planet. We've also identified several missile batteries and a couple of satellites. The data shows that the enemy cruisers are protected by over-laying fields of fire from the various bases. There also appear to be minefields protecting the orbiting ships and the approaches to the bases."

Gallant said, "The combination of cruisers and missile bases outguns Neumann's force by a consider-able margin."

"We need to notify Commander Neumann," said McCall.

"OOD, send an updated sighting report to *Achilles*.," said Gallant.

Several of the officers shifted in their seats, ex-changing uncomfortable glances.

"Our original orders were to scout ahead of the force and evaluate the Titan ships and bases. This large increase in ships is not only unexcepted but troublesome. We should remain in stealth mode and await new orders," said Roberts.

"On the contrary, I intend to move the *Warrior* behind the fifth planet. From there, we can send the Wasp to the moon base and tap into their commu-nications network. I may be able to penetrate their defense network and get valuable information," said Gallant.

Roberts and several other officers nodded en-thusiastically.

It was many hours before the *Achilles* finally re-sponded. By that time, Gallant had already infiltrated the Titan moon base's communication network. He set up a fake identity and gained access to several sensitive computer-controlled areas. Next, he identified the networks for both the sensor arrays and the missile batteries. Soon, he gained access to their controls.

When the Wasp returned to the *Warrior*, he met with McCall and Roberts in CIC.

Roberts said, "The *Achilles* and its four destroyers are on their way to join us. Based on his communication, I gather Commander Neumann means to fight ship-to-ship, despite the odds."

"Maybe we can even those odds up a bit," said Gallant.

McCall asked, "What do you mean?"

"I think I can distort the base's sensors to keep them from identifying the *Achilles* task force as it approaches."

"That would give them the element of surprise," said Roberts approvingly, "and definitely improve our chances."

Through his fake identity, Gallant manipulated the base's sensor data to disguise the *Achilles* task force's signal. It would now appear as one large natural object. It was a simple matter of size and clarity. Contrasting the transparency of space against material bodies, it wasn't difficult to match objects of the *Achilles'* size. He merely introduced sensor input data that resembled a comet and overlaid it on the *Achilles'* readings.

Gallant reported the deception to Neumann, who acknowledged the tactic without comment.

As part of his preparations, Gallant examined

the Titan defenses in greater detail. The bases had a layered defense system that included satellites, minefields, and overlapping fields of fire. There were scores of missile launchers guarding the approaches. Still, as he studied the Titan system, he became convinced that he could gain control over some of the base missile batteries.

When Neumann's ships approached the planet, ready to close in on the enemy, Gallant requested permission to proceed with his plan. After an extended wait, Neumann gave him permission.

The *Warrior* remained in stealth mode behind the fifth planet while Gallant and Stedman, took the Wasp to the junction box. There, Gallant, as he had on the Titan world, connected into the master circuit via his neural network. Using his fake identity, he introduced a virus that locked up the missile battery controls.

"The missile bases' defense systems are no longer operational," reported Gallant to the *Achilles*. Neumann didn't respond.

Although Gallant had disabled the weapons' sensors and defenses, he wasn't able to access the cruisers' internal networks. The aliens would be able to fight at full capacity once they realized that the *Achilles* was upon them.

The four Titan ships orbited the large moon, oblivious to the approach of their foe. Because the bases' sensors remained distorted, the *Achilles* took the aliens by surprise.

Neumann didn't fire as soon as the Titan ships recognized the enemy and scrambled into defensive postures. He held his punch.

When he was satisfied that his force was at optimal range, he ordered, "Attack. Repeat, attack. All ships launch missiles on designated targets."

The *Achilles* and its destroyers had preselected individual cruisers to target, and the first salvo of twenty-four missiles was launched at optimal range with great precision. Six missiles per cruiser—each multi-warhead missile with a dozen thermonuclear devices—rained down on the Titan ships.

Expecting the base defenses to protect them, the cruisers didn't immediately respond to the incoming missiles. By the time they realized their external defense had failed, they didn't have time to deploy any decoys. The best they could manage was a ragged anti-missile barrage, which prevented the complete destruction Neumann had hoped for. Several of the warheads made direct hits on their targets. In one blow, the *Achilles* task force destroyed one cruiser and critically damaged another.

Neumann's force now had a fair chance in a toe-to-toe slugging match with the remaining Titan ships.

But the Titans were known to be resourceful and contentious. They would seek retaliation.

Meantime, the *Warrior* remained in stealth mode on the far side of the planet, awaiting Gallant's return. He traversed the moon's surface as fast as he could in the low gravity. Uppermost in his mind was the knowledge that he must not delay an instant in getting the *Warrior* into the battle.

The *Achilles* and its four destroyers charged headlong at the remaining enemy cruisers without waiting.

The Titans were quick to respond. A flurry of missiles headed toward at the *Achilles*.

One destroyer, the *Fletcher*, maneuvered to shield the *Achilles* from the incoming missiles. She exploded in a fiery ball, leaving nothing but a shower of debris on the viewscreens.

Several of the remaining missiles bypassed to reach the *Achilles'* countermeasures, and she suffered considerable damage from near misses.

Neumann signaled, "All ships close on the enemy."

Settling into attack formation, the Titan cruisers tore through space directly toward the *Achilles* task force.

Gallant was desperate to join the battle. He docked the Wasp with the *Warrior* and ordered an intercept course for the enemy ships. But the *Warrior*

was significantly out of position and a good distance from the action, and because the enemy cruisers were moving directly away from him, it would be at least thirty minutes before he could engage.

"Red-alert message from *Achilles*, sir," said the OOD.

"Read it aloud."

"Engage the enemy. Repeat, engage the enemy."

Gallant cursed.

Neumann was a fool to engage at close range without waiting for the Warrior.

Pushing the regrets away, Gallant ordered, "Engineering, red-line the engines. Chief Howard, I want everything you can give me and then some."

He estimated that despite all he had done, the odds against the *Achilles* were still long.

"Helm, lock on to the nearest Titan ship, and match its maneuvers."

The *Warrior* accelerated toward the battle, even as the action moved away from them.

The *Achilles* task force fired another salvo, destroying the crippled cruiser and damaging one of the two remaining cruisers.

Then CIC reported, "Enemy cruisers have launched a salvo at the *Achilles.* She's already damaged, barely able to navigate, let alone defend herself. Her destroyer escort is forming a defensive line and firing antimissiles."

Gallant watched the exchange helplessly. The antimissiles destroyed several of the incoming missiles, but enough got through and another destroyer exploded. The *Achilles* was irreparably damaged, trying to limp out of range. Gallant cringed at the destruction.

"Red-alert message from the *Achilles*, sir."

"Read it."

Neumann called out the *Warrior* explicitly for admonishment over an open channel. "*Warrior* engage the enemy. Repeat, engage the enemy."

Gallant flushed bright red. From the outset of the action, a man on board the *Warrior* was ignorant of the need to close on the enemy cruisers. The crew was prickling to get at them, but physics determined their approach.

"Weapons, how long until we reach our maximum weapons envelope?"

"Seven minutes, sir. But that's stretching it."

"Engineering, increase engine power."

Howard responded, "Sir, we're well past the redline, at 120 percent power already."

A desperate compromise formed in Gallant's mind. He said, "Overload reactors, allow limited core damage, evacuate the engineering spaces with the exception of the emergency response team, and initiate radiation protection protocol throughout the ship."

"Aye aye, sir."

"Helm, continue on course to intercept the nearest Titan cruiser."

"Aye aye, sir."

Over the comm system, Gallant heard, "Bridge, starboard reactor is overheated and approaching a meltdown."

Gallant recognized the strain in Chief Howard's voice. He and four volunteers had remained in engineering while the rest of the team evacuated.

"Engineering, initiate emergency radiation protocol," ordered Gallant. Now, he couldn't spare any thought to consider the fate of those men, even Howard, who was the closest thing to a father he had ever known. This battle had taken on a fantastic unreality, a never-ending nightmare in which he was running in slow motion, unable to move forward.

The two remaining enemy cruisers launched another devastating salvo at the *Achilles.* She suffered more and more damage.

Again, the *Warrior* received a direct order from the *Achilles*: "*Warrior*, engage the enemy more closely. Repeat, engage the enemy more closely."

The *Warrior* was nearly in range when Gallant heard, "Bridge, the second reactor is overheating. Core meltdown is imminent."

Gallant heard the report, and his hopes waned. He knew Howard must be desperate to make the report at this critical time.

As the *Warrior* finally drew within weapons range, he ordered, "Helm, reduce speed to standard."

Then, "Weapons, commence firing!"

His eyes darted around the battle scene, taking in the ships, the missiles, and their trajectories. With the *Achilles* on one side of the enemy and the *Warrior* on the other, the Titan's would have to decide which course to take.

They came around and headed at the *Warrior*.

"Humph," said Gallant watching the enemy bearing down on him. A wave of apprehension and excitement didn't stop him from calculating his next course of action. He swallowed hard and set his plan of action in motion.

Because the *Achilles* was no longer able to respond to communications, he directed his ship's fire. He managed to concentrate their missile salvo at the weak spots of the two remaining cruisers while the *Warrior's* high energy cannon spat at the foe.

Each side approached unwaveringly as both sides recharged their weapons. The destroyer remained on the starboard side of the *Achilles* to shield her.

Both Titan cruisers were severely damaged but launched their last missiles from a parallel course with the *Warrior,* aiming one at the *Warrior* and the other toward the *Achilles*.

The missile flight time was a mere twenty seconds, and it didn't allow time to deploy decoys or countermeasures. It completely disrupted their organization. The UP destroyers attempted to knock them down with antimissiles. Instead of firing a return salvo, the UP ships spent several confused minutes avoiding collisions while evading the incoming missiles. The devastating accuracy of the missile fire was disheartening to watch.

The destroyers launched another small salvo of missiles. As the UP's missiles approached their target, the aliens deployed countermeasures. Antimissile missiles from the Titans were in the path of the remaining missiles. Nevertheless, Gallant distinguished half-dozen explosions. One cruiser exploded, and the remaining Titan cruiser was disabled.

As the battle ebbed and flowed, only one Titan cruiser remained. But it had a greater impact on the UP ships. The battle was only one hour old, and thousands had already died. The *Achilles'* position was sunward of the lone remaining enemy cruiser. She was engaging closely but was taking a terrible pounding. To her credit, she was beating up on the Titans too.

The last Titan fired two missiles, which greatly contributed to the confusion of battle when the thermonuclear firestorm erupted around the *Warrior*.

A word from Gallant swung the *Warrior* toward the last enemy ship. The ships were now fighting in the clinches with their remaining lasers and plasma weapons.

Roberts said, "Their fire is slackening."

The *Warrior* moved ahead, and the cruiser came upon their larboard quarter. Both ships continued firing until the cruiser reached the *Achilles*. When she had gained a sufficient distance, it raked them and the enemy launched a single missile.

Gallant fumed while the *Warrior* was unable to bring a single weapon to bear upon the cruiser.

The cruiser bore around hard and ran toward the *Achilles*. The ships were extremely close, and they used their secondary weapons to light up the enemy. The nuclear warheads damaged the cruiser's forward shield and ruptured its forward missile compartment.

They separated momentarily and turned to re-engage, even more fiercely than before. Nothing deterred them.

Gallant ordered the destroyers to launch an all-out counterattack, charging straight at the Titan ships and launching missiles. Still, the Titan cruiser streamed forward.

Gallant hoped the *Achilles* could hold on a little while longer. He tried to balance in his mind the calculus of ships lost on each side, to reach a conclusion that he could accept.

The weapons fire from the *Warrior* was conducted with so much skill and effect that the enemy cruiser finally turned aside.

"Bridge, three of the volunteers who stayed in engineering, have died of radiation poisoning. Chief Howard and the other men are critically ill in the med center."

"Very well."

Gallant was puzzled for a moment, his ship's propulsion likely to fail at any moment. Sucking in a deep breath, he considered a plan of attack. Three of the UP destroyers were lost. The *Achilles* was out of action, and only one destroyer remained to support the *Warrior* against the single crippled Titan cruiser.

The last cruiser limped around, preparing for another attack.

Gallant maneuvered into position and ordered long-range shots with the FASER.

After exchanging several shots and knocking

out the enemy missiles, the last UP destroyer veered away. She'd had enough. She was so severely damaged that she could no longer fight but could only look for a means to escape.

The power of the Titan's missiles was now set against the *Warrior's* high-energy cannon. One weapon dwarfed in scale, the other in results.

He was now engaged in a desperate battle with the remaining damaged Titan cruiser.

A missile exploded nearby, then another. He leaped to his feet after falling from his chair. He dry-heaved.

Gallant had to make a rapid decision and live with the consequences...

Courage will only get you so far. Use your head.

The *Warrior* had sustained significant damage from the last missile. Atmosphere was leaking out from a hull crack. Smoke drifted across the bridge and wafted through the corridors trailing noxious fumes. Alarms flashed warnings about imminent environmental systems failure.

Gallant raged against the Titans. Following the only course of action, he kept his ship fighting, firing whatever weapons remained. The *Warrior* would not falter from lack of courage or determination.

The *Achilles* had been drifting, almost forgotten. But the *Warrior* had afforded her time to regroup. She set her target and launched one last round of missiles at the Titan cruiser.

They were enough.

The warheads exploded against the enemy

cruiser, sending out a plasma shock wave that rattled the *Warrior*, the *Achilles,* and the destroyer. All that remained was debris drifting in space near the fifth planet of Tau Ceti.

It wasn't until Gallant received a message from the only remaining officer on the *Achilles*, Ensign McDermott, that he learned that Neumann had died in the last encounter.

The damaged ships limped back to Elysium, struggling to repair damaged systems, and treating the many wounded.

The explosions burned Chief Howard's body. Several of his internal organs were ruptured and had to be reconstructed. He had at least eight serious wounds and numerous minor ones. It took many hours of surgery to reconstruct him into something worth keeping. Oxygen conduits, blood tubes, and electrical wires were connected to a multitude of locations on his body—mouth, nose, veins—allowing chemicals and nano-bots to be pumped throughout his blood and endocrine systems to revitalize him and restore hope for his survival. The nano-bots traveled throughout his body, conducting pre-programmed internal microsurgery and cell repairs. Electrical sensors were wired to his temple to control his brain functions, and others were connected to his heart and lungs. The surgeon performed a skin graft and cut away dead tissue suffering from radiation burns. The effort was enough to keep Howard alive.

Lying in his regeneration chamber, he listened to all the activity around him. There was a good deal of chatter about reaching Elysium and the plans the crew had for liberty. He was weak as a kitten but eager to get up and about even though he was sewn together in long swatches, and the slightest movement was painful. He heard the med techs muttering about a big wig doctor from Halo coming to personally tend him when they landed—thanks to a personal request from Alaina Hepburn.

He would have welcomed any activity even in his current state. He fidgeted and wriggled, trying to get comfortable, but to no avail.

The ship seemed oddly quiet when Gallant came into his room and chuckled.

"Begging your pardon, sir, I don't see anything to laugh about," said Howard petulantly. He shifted uncomfortably in the regeneration chamber.

"Of course, Chief," said Gallant, though his smile broadened. "There's nothing at all to laugh about."

"Then kindly remove that grin . . . sir," Howard grumbled.

"Anything else?" asked Gallant, pulling his face into a scowl, though the corners of his mouth twitched suspiciously.

"No, sir."

"Then I'll get back to my duties."

Left to himself again, Howard swore under his breath. He'd intended to ask the captain about the ship's condition. Even locked in a regeneration chamber, he hated inactivity, hated not knowing what was happening.

A med-tech came in with a variety of fruits.

"Captain's compliments," said a petty officer carrying a basket of fruit. "He thought you'd like to know, we're approaching Elysium."

"Please pass my thanks on to the captain."

"Sure, Chief."

He bit into some of the soft fruit and enjoyed the sweet juices on his tongue. He paused between bites when he heard Gallant's voice outside his room.

A new doctor entered. He examined Howard with a critical eye.

"I'm sure you've seen worse than me?" queried Howard.

"No, actually, you have significant injuries, though the med team has done good work on you. You're on the mend. Sorry, but I need to examine you more thoroughly."

"Dammit!" Howard let loose a string of invective.

"I'll give you something for the pain, but you'll have to handle your foul temper yourself."

Gallant chuckled again, and again Howard snorted.

Gallant suppressed the laugh, but a grin remained on his face.

CHAPTER 27

Winner Take All

A week after the Titans were defeated and Commander Neumann died aboard the Achilles, the people of Halo rejoiced. The *Warrior* arrived at Elysium with the remaining United Planets ships.

Aboard the *Warrior*, Gallant was seated comfortably in his cabin when a knock was followed by the door swinging open.

Commander Julie Ann McCall waltzed in and plopped down on his cot. Her bright smile was accompanied by a sweep of her fingers running through her hair.

"Make yourself comfortable," said Gallant with a smirk.

"I always do," she laughed.

"What can I do for you, Commander?"

McCall said, "Strange as it may seem, you are now the senior United Planets line-officer. You are in command of the damaged *Achilles*, the remaining destroyers, and the *Warrior*. In addition, you are the acting governor of Elysium."

To Gallant's surprise, her reaction toward him showed a new-found respect. She still had a dominating personality, but for now she was willing to defer to his authority.

He said, "Yes, I am all that. And my first order of business is to appoint Lieutenant Roberts as commander of the *Achilles*. I will leave the headache of that ship's repairs to him. I hope that meets with your approval."

"Of course. But I suggest that you deal with the political situation here on Elysium immediately."

"As soon as we reached orbit, I dispatched military police to round up Wolfe and his rowdies. I am issuing an executive order to hold an election in two weeks so the citizens can vote for new leadership."

"Will that include *universal* suffrage."

"Absolutely," said Gallant. "But I shouldn't be surprised if Liam wins."

"Possibly."

"In any case, I am rescinding Neumann's mandate for genetic engineering. The people can decide for themselves how to direct their future."

"All well and good, but Elysium's future will have to wait until we deal with Neumann's powerful father. He could still work to reverse everything."

"He's far away, and the situation here will become settled before long."

"You're optimistic."

"Hopeful. Just hopeful"

McCall tilted her head to one side and asked with a sly smile, "Isn't there some personal business you still have to attend to?"

CHAPTER 28

The Question

Gallant read the words of Alaina's letter again. She wanted to see him. He didn't want to presume too much. The note was not romantic. It included an apology for intruding on his busy schedule and a few words expressing her hope that he was well.

Anxious, he went to her home.

Alaina was beautiful, and never more so than now.

She greeted him with a coy, "Maybe you thought yourself well rid of me? Or perhaps you've been restless to return? I hope it was the latter."

"I've thought of no one else." He ached to hold her but clasped his hands behind his back instead.

"Are you well?"

"Yes. We fought a battle with terrible losses, but yes, I am well," said Gallant, tugging at his collar.

He told her something about his mission. He

began slowly, but then the words poured out of him—words of excitement, possibilities, and potential disaster. When he had run out of things to say, they sat for what seemed like a long time. The tension of their last meeting melted away into a comfortable silence, and they began to chat about mundane things.

It was incredible, the many things he spoke of, and she responded in kind—two old friends catching up. He felt the same way every time he saw her after a long absence—he fell under her spell all over again.

When the conversation paused again, she shifted to face him and looked into his eyes.

"I wish to hear more—but later. For now, I'm interested in you and me. Can we talk of us?" she asked.

He'd learned that his rational approach could be an encumbrance when dealing with emotional issues, but he liked that she was open and without pretense.

"Yes. Let's talk about us." Gallant asked the question that had been at the forefront of his mind since he arrived, "So, you aren't married? Nothing is settled?"

"No."

A wave of relief washed over him.

As the past flowed into the present—repeating the most perplexing events of his life—Gallant was with Alaina, wanting things he was uncertain could ever be. He knew beyond doubt that exceptional people help focus one's life along a path—they hold an emotional lock on one's being. For him, Alaina was one of those people. Simply seeing her again unlocked all his memories and unleashed all his passion. He had often imagined this rendezvous, but at this moment, he couldn't speak. He had a burning desire to let loose his innermost feelings, yet he felt confused and tongue-tied. Was it possible that he had some essential character defect? What else could explain why he, normally so competent and self-assured, became dumbstruck and graceless in her presence?

His dilemma remained—as always—could he and Alaina find a future together?

Their past felt like loose strings wound together, a series of unrelated events twisted into a tangled knot. Gallant could pull on any strand to start a conversation, but that would only tighten the knot. That approach would never free them to start over.

Instead of speaking, he took hold of her shoulders and looked searchingly into her eyes. He breathed in her scent. She was intoxicating. Their awkward position mirrored their emotions.

He put his hand on her cheek. She leaned forward, resting her head on his chest. She slid her hand around the nape of his neck, as if pulling him in for a kiss, but at the last moment, she hesitated.

"Last time, I pushed you away," she said, "when I should have held fast."

In her eyes, in her touch, he felt her desire, and he swept her into his arms.

As they kissed, the world around them spun away and disappeared.

He spoke, the words whispered from deep in

his heart, "Alaina, I've loved you for so long. I can't lose you again. The most painful regrets in life are those where you had a choice. I won't make the wrong choice."

"Are you giving me a choice now?"

"Yes."

She said, "There are so many uncertainties facing us, coming from every direction. I don't know what to do."

"I love you, Alaina. I want you. That's all that matters."

"I'm insanely in love with you, Henry."

For a moment, she looked like she would cry.

He pulled her close once more. They kissed again, a deep passionate kiss, filled with longing and desire.

"Oh, Henry, Henry, Henry, what are we to do?"

Gallant said, "I've struggled to make sense of my life, but I still don't have the answers. Ah, why does love have to be so bewildering?"

With an expansive smile, she replied, "It's really not so bewildering. You just have to love the other person more than yourself."

Gallant's eyes opened wide.

"Alaina, I love you. Marry me, and we'll face whatever comes—together. Just say yes."

"Yes."

—the end—

FROM THE AUTHOR

I hope you enjoyed this book. I must confess—I'm proud of my characters and the story they tell. Henry and Alaina are bold, brave, and possess a sense of humor—qualities I admire. Their story is rich with a belief in personal responsibility and honor.

If you have a comment, please post a review on Amazon.

H. Peter Alesso.

For notification of future books click the Follow button on the author page.

Amazon Author: H. Peter Alesso

Book 5 in the Henry Gallant Saga,

CAPTAIN HENRY GALLANT

Henry Gallant is the captain of the spacecraft carrier *Constellation*. He is the last hope of the Marines stranded on a volcanic wasteland nine light-years from Earth.

Not since Guadalcanal has the 2nd Marine Division faced a grimmer struggle to hold on against a powerful and ruthless enemy.

As the Titan invaders close in, the Marines wonder if there is the 'will' to save them.

Top Gun pilots Rob Ryan and Lorelei Steward take a desperate gamble to save Nathan Steward and the remnants of the 2nd Division.

Will they be in time?

Will they be enough?

For fans of Honor Harrington and Horatio Hornblower.

61267768R00132